Stranger in the Shadows

Acknowledgments

There are many people to thank when writing a book.

Thank you to my best friends Kylie and Melissa. For understanding me ghosting for weeks so I was able to write and always having the best gossip when I needed a break. You two are such a constant in my life.

To the fabulous Rosie. The best editor, writer, and friend all rolled into one person. You are irreplaceable, and I love you so.

To the best grandparents in the world. For telling me to shoot for the stars, for being a breath of fresh air on my worst days, and for being role models of incredible strength.

Thank you to my sisters, who inspired these stories. You are my safe haven. I couldn't have picked better girls to grow up with. To all the people who have bought a book, read one of the proofs, or talked me through a tough scene, I am indebted to you forever.

Last, but not least, thank you to my husband and children. Mason and Torie, you are my greatest adventures and are the best part of my day. Thyler, you are my favorite person in the world, and you make all of my dreams possible. Forever is not enough.

For Viola,

No matter where in the world you are.

Chapter 1

My doctor warned me that I might have holes in my memory after waking up from my coma. He told me I might lose pieces of days and maybe even years. But that didn't seem to be the problem.

I remembered everything. I saw myself go through surgery; I saw the breathing tube shoved down my throat and still woke up fighting it long after it was removed. I remembered CJ lying next to me and playing me song after song. I remember Claire and Macy climbing into bed with me and wrapping my lifeless arms around them in hope.

I also remembered another body, another time period. I remember looking in the mirror and seeing thick brown braids curling down my back instead of the red pixie cut I have sported since college. I saw brown eyes with huge lashes looking back at me instead of the silky green I was accustomed to.

I remembered a different house and knew that I belonged to that time just as much as I belonged to today. Another family that I loved. Their names tasted easy on my tongue and being with them felt as natural as breathing. I had another someone I loved and had planned a life with.

These memories felt like home, my soul coming full circle and uncovering a part of me that had tried to leave itself behind. All of this seemed normal somehow. As if I had carried this other self around with me my whole life. Yet, these weren't the only memories I carried.

A memory of plunging a knife into a man's chest over and over, my palms becoming slick with blood. Looking into his shocked expression until I saw the life drain out. Nothing else describes how the light can just be snuffed out of another person's body. One second, they are fighting for breath. The next they are just a shell.

I remember washing my hands in the sink and wincing at the claw marks on the inside of my arms and scoring my knuckles. But worst of all, I remember looking into the mirror and smiling. I remember feeling more satisfied than I ever thought possible.

*

"You don't have to take this stuff now. I'm sure you will be back before you know it," Lucy told me.

She was holding a book from my shelf in her arms as if she could physically keep me from leaving.

I sighed, sitting back in the orthopedic chair my mom had bought for my office when I first got my job at the Spokane Women's Center. This was a million times more comfortable than the purple padded seat of the walker that I had to haul around now. The pad was already worn from constant use over the last few months.

However, even this office chair brought back a million painful memories that I didn't want to deal with. Instead, I chose to remember the day my mom hauled this over to me my first week of work. My mom knew me so well, the chair was even lime green.

A tightening crept over my chest as I thought of my mom. She kept coming back at me in the present tense this way. I kept having to remind myself that I wasn't going back home to her.

"It's a leave of absence, Lucy. I will be back. But until then, I am going to set up an office at home. Just until I get back up on my feet."

"Terry is healing from a traumatic brain injury, Luc. She will heal and kick butt at physical therapy, and she will be back before you know it," Macy nodded, attempting to reassure me.

Macy smiled at Lucy as she put all of my folders into the filing cabinet. It was a quiet dismissal, and I loved her for it.

Lucy nodded, releasing the book then heading back out to her desk.

I really did feel terrible that she was upset. She was my secretary, and her job was hanging in a weird balance until I figured out what I was going to do. But just being in this office was too much for me.

Last year a patient of mine murdered her mother and boyfriend. Her case was looming on the horizon, and I was set to testify against her. So, for right now, I am not capable of this role.

Ever since I got out of the hospital, my heart pulsed like a massive open wound. I couldn't just sit across from a woman in crisis and pretend like their pain wasn't poisoning the rest of my life. I had gotten lost in Gina, and I wasn't sure I was ever going to find my way back.

It wasn't just my confidence that had taken a hit. The women that came here were aware of my being a future witness in the case and would have to think twice before fully trusting me. It was a considerable feat to come to the center and lay all of their secrets bare. How could they talk to me when I was uncovering the secrets of a former patient?

I wanted to be trusted, but right now the last thing I wanted to do was pretend like I had my shit together.

I am terrified of the women now. Even now sitting at my desk, I can feel their desperation and hear the cry of their past trauma pushing into my mind. I see the woman scrubbing blood out of her clothes so that her neighbors won't notice. I can taste the metallic shower bar that broke another woman's front teeth just days before. I feel the punches across my cheekbones and knees in my stomach. How am I supposed to help anyone if I can't separate their bruises from my own?

Gina's case was a statewide sensation. Her smothering her mother had rocked our city. All the newspapers wanted to know what lead to her nervous breakdown. What caused a person to reach that kind of low in their psyche? Her lawyer was probably banking on battered women's syndrome, but she was much more than the broken woman I believed her to be.

Everyone wanted the truth, but I didn't even know where to start. What I couldn't say to all of those vulnerable people out there was that I had trusted Gina. It was my job to listen and believe her because no one else did. She took that confidence and twisted it until it became an alibi.

I learned that victims come in many forms. Villains could hide inside of someone who seemed helpless. I thought she was broken and helped her nurse her wounds. She ended up being the wolf all along.

"Well, that's it," I say to Macy, pulling my walker closer so that I was able to stand up. It took way longer than I wanted it too and I had to force myself not to grimace.

I stared at my feet, willing them to help me walk out of here with my dignity intact. My entire body weighed me down like a bag full of wet sand. No amount of willpower helped me move the way my mind wanted to. Macy started to come towards me, and I shook my head at her. I took a deep breath and began my painful shuffle.

Lucy met us at her desk. She touched my cheek like she was saying goodbye. "Feel better, Terry. Come back to us, we need you."

Macy hugged her and picked up two boxes, lagging behind so that she could keep an eye on me. I nodded at Lucy but didn't respond. I stayed in the lobby for a half a second, frozen.

I didn't want to be home any more than I wanted to be here. In my office, I couldn't get thoughts of Gina out of my mind and was trapped in my patient's fears. But at home, I will eventually have to accept the fact that my mom wasn't coming back. I would have to admit that she was really dead. I hung my head and made my way out of the center. My failure followed me out to my car, where Macy deposited the remainder of my career in the trunk. I carefully folded myself into the passenger seat and then finally let myself cry.

*

"Anything else on the grocery list?" Macy asked, holding a pen over her hot pink pad of paper.

Claire nodded towards the dish soap I was using to wash the dishes. "More Dawn. I bought a two pack, but I think we are on the last one."

Macy wrote it down, and I struggled to have something to add as well. I didn't want Claire to be in charge of running our house or start to change the way that things had been done in the past. I needed to get back to my life, which included being the one to take care of my sisters. The more she stepped up, the more I was reminded that I was just a shadow of my former self.

I didn't feel like a fully functioning member of our household right now. I couldn't contribute anything. I wasn't even able to do the dishes. I was sitting on my walker, and my arms trembled as I ran the sponge over four plates. There was no way I was going to be able to tackle the pots and put them in the sink to soak instead.

"Maybe some shampoo?" I asked, not turning around.

"No, I picked up some yesterday while Ash and I were at Costco. There was no room in the bathroom, I put it in the laundry room," Claire told me.

I froze, irrational anger tingling in my fingertips.

"Mom never put shampoo in the laundry room."

Macy looked at me curiously.

"Are you okay?" Claire asked me, touching my arm lightly.

I knew she was working really hard to support me, but my head still swam with anger whenever I looked at her. Waking up and seeing my sister had filled me with such peace. For one minute, 60 seconds of bliss before finding out that my mom was gone. That they had buried her without me.

It wasn't Claire's fault, but being the oldest, even for just the summer, wasn't all fun and games. She was the only person I was able to give this pain to.

"I'm fine."

Macy sat down. "You really seem like you aren't here all the way. Have you been having headaches or anything? Your doctor said we might need to watch out for neurological changes."

She and Claire shared a look. I had tried talking to them about the new memories I had while in the hospital. They were convinced that it was a side effect of my coma and Macy kept trying to hint that my aura seemed damaged. The visions were real, and I wanted to share it with them, but I was tired of feeling like I was crazy.

I sighed and sat down, knowing that she would keep trying to look into my aura if I didn't give her anything.

"I have been having some more... dreams."

"What kind of dreams?" Claire asked, her eyes clouded with concern.

A knife slick in blood flashed through my mind. I shook the thoughts away and settled on the memories I had begun having most recently. Of loving a man named Kerry. His lips and how it felt to have his fingers running up and down my body.

"She was in love. Sometimes it feels like he is still here and that finding this part of myself helped wake me up. These aren't dreams. I have been having visions of it, of her."

They shared one more look then seemed to deflate and agree to just humor me. I didn't care if they believed me or not. I just needed to talk about it.

Macy looked at me dreamily, seeming relieved that the secret I was keeping was just about a boy.

"That's kind of romantic."

Claire's cheeks reddened. "What about CJ?"

I looked away from her, blushing myself. When I thought of CJ, guilt climbed up my throat like a sickness. Seeing him now filled my head with music, the same music that was weaved through our shared history. I knew he took care of me like a lover, like his other half.

I looked back at my sister. The kitchen had changed ever so slightly. Bills on the counter addressed to my mom. Keys in the drawer to an office that I was afraid of calling mine. A calendar with court dates written on it.

I loved CJ, but the appeal of escaping with Kerry was too tempting. He loved me and being here and figuring all of this out on my own was too painful.

Claire

Last June I lost a lot of things. I lost my veil entirely and began seeing ghosts. I had always been the normal one in my family, and it was something that I had held onto to the point of self-destruction. Setting myself apart had cheated me out of a close relationship with my sisters, and I lost my mom after a horrific car accident. To bring her justice, I was reckless with my gift. I let ghosts in without guarding myself and had allowed shadow figures into our home and into my mind.

I was finally able to contact my mother from the other side, and she was teaching me to put up boundaries. She told me that I needed to build a relationship with a spirit guide so that they would be my go-between with ghosts that I wasn't ready to talk to.

Yet, I wasn't committing to these boundaries as much as I should. I was barely able to hold onto my connection with my mom, and I wasn't ready to say goodbye to her yet. I was still repairing over five years of selfishness, I still felt like such a fraud whenever my sisters hugged me. I hated myself a little bit and sometimes wondered if they did too.

I lost myself as a writer entirely because I was telling stories I had no right to put on paper. I had begun outlining my second novel, but it was like I was pulling out my own teeth with children's pliers. Were these actual characters or more lost people?

I shut my laptop, letting out a breath and giving up on work for the night. I slipped off my socks and covered myself up. As I turned off the light, I saw a figure blocking out the glow from the hallway. The figures were getting more robust and moved faster than ever.

There were so many times that I woke up surrounded by them as they leaned over the side of my bed. I took a deep breath, imagining a brick wall inside of myself the way that my mom had taught me. I built the fortress brick by brick until it was as real as the sheets underneath me.

Building a wall in my mind wasn't the only thing that helped these days. I had found strength in love as well. The summer ended with losing my heart completely. Holden had not just stolen it; he had done it so quickly and quietly that I couldn't remember a time he wasn't by my side. For the first time in my life, I was able to picture my future and allow someone to share it with me. He made me brave and feel beautiful. He made the darkness go away and gave the light a reason to shine.

*

"Pass the ketchup please," Macy mumbled, staring at her phone instead of her plate as we ate.

I passed it and concentrated on choking down the sweet potato fries Terry had made. She was on a health kick recently and was making sweet potatoes instead of pasta at least twice a week. I have hated them since we were kids and had a feeling that Terry knew that.

We usually alternated making dinner, and she was teaching me how to be a passable cook. It should have felt like a bonding moment, but it was like having to adjust to living here all over again. When Terry was first released from the hospital, I assumed that she wanted me to stay until she was strong.

Now that she was okay, I had to ask for permission to live here with them from now on. But it didn't seem like a temporary fix to me anymore. I wasn't able to picture myself anywhere else. I was supposed to be here. But I had a feeling that Terry didn't share those same dreams with me anymore.

Macy and I had all summer to grieve our mom's death in our own way, but Terry was facing her pain for the first time. One night I had woken up to her bawling in the kitchen because I had moved the coffee pot to the other counter to make room for a new bread box. Mom had organized the kitchen and having me move anything was devastating to her. She told me that I was erasing pieces of her before she had a chance to say goodbye.

I went back to being a half guest. I cleaned my dishes as soon as I was done eating, so she didn't see a plate that didn't belong. I left my mom's cups in the cupboard and used the mugs that I bought while in college. I separated my laundry and left Mom's door shut.

I loved my sisters and had no idea how to prove myself to them. Terry promised me that she didn't blame anyone but Lucas for the accident, but she refused to look at me whenever we brought it up.

"There's a bonfire tonight at Shayla's. Do you care if I go?" Macy asked, turning to Terry.

Terry glanced at the clock. "It's already 7. That doesn't extend your curfew. Go, but be back by 11."

Macy nodded and grabbed the car keys from the ring. "Sounds good. Don't stay up too late."

Terry laughed, making me giggle as well. "Yeah. Not happening. I'll see you at 11."

Terry shook her head as Macy glided out of the house and to the car. She never seemed to fully touch the ground and instead pranced around on her tiptoes like she was a fairy getting ready to take flight. I always felt like I was tethering her to the moment and to the earth one way or another.

"What do you think they do at bonfires in 12th grade? I feel like I missed those days. I was always too busy chasing after Ken to keep him from cheating on me."

"I don't even want to know. Sometimes I am glad she's into girls because that keeps me from worrying about her getting pregnant. But it doesn't stop her from drinking too much or doing whatever else is offered. She's never gotten into serious trouble before, so I try just to trust her."

I nodded, going back to my plate. Something about the way that Terry told me about Macy rubbed me the wrong way. I didn't need to be told about her. I knew her. I was the one who had taken care of her for the past four months. I had confronted Dad for her, helped her move on from her pain, and get ready for her senior year. Was it too much to ask for thanks? Was it too much to want to be recognized for how much I had changed?

*

"Is this the place?" Holden asked, turning down the music in his truck.

I sat up and looked around. We idled by a marker to the lake that we had frequented during high school.

"Yep, you really have never been here?" I asked.

"I didn't say that. I said the last time I came here I was already drunk, and Ken drove us. I was asleep on the way home. I remember a lake. I remember puking in some bushes. I remember waking up in my own bed still wearing sneakers covered in mud."

I hopped out and reached for his hand as he met me in front of his truck.

"Well, let's make some better memories then."

I led him around the lake. As we wrapped around towards the farthest edge of the water, the ground rose and fell. I loved hiking growing up. Whenever we went camping, I always disappeared behind the campground and tried to find places that weren't listed on the camp website. It's easy to locate the creek the area is famous for, but it's special to see the waterfall that locals kept a secret. This one wasn't even marked by a sign.

"What did you do when you came here in high school?" Holden asked, pulling me close to peck me on the cheek.

"Mostly, I just sat alone. I was either waiting for Ken or watching him get drunk and flirt with everyone that wasn't me. It was humiliating. It was like everyone knew that I was the one who loved him more and they all thought I was pathetic for holding on when he apparently didn't feel the same."

"Then why did you?"

Holden sat down and stretched his legs out in front of him on a boulder that overlooked the lake below.

I sat next to him and let my feet dangle.

"When we were alone, he was different. When it was just the two of us, he looked at me like he understood my heart. Or, understood me as well as anyone could when I was a sixteen-year-old. He told me that I was beautiful. That sounds dumb, but it meant so much to me. He saw all of me in a way no one else had up until that point and loved it anyway."

"From what I remember, you were beautiful back then. Why wouldn't he love you?"

I tried not to look at him. Holden always seemed to be able to cut through the bullshit and get me to say things I had never spoken out loud before.

"Maybe I didn't love myself very much back then. Anyone thinking I was worthy of their time meant something because I didn't find myself very worthy."

Holden leaned over squeezed my knee, and I was grateful that he didn't attempt to hug me instead. He never tried to make me feel better about things from back then. He seemed to know that pushing too hard made me want to close myself off. Holden just listening and reaching out meant the world to me because it was just what I needed.

I bumped him with my shoulder. "I was beautiful back then?"

Holden laughed. "Well yeah. You were beautiful then. You're gorgeous now."

I snorted. "What a line. You really wanted me to comment so that you could say that. How long were you keeping that one to yourself?"

Holden put his forehead against mine. "You know me too well. I thought of that a week ago while we were at dinner and talking about reunions. I am pretty smooth if I say so myself."

I gently kneaded my fingers through his hair and pulled him closer. "I say so too."

As we kissed Holden inevitably pulled me into his lap. I stood up instead, smiling.

"Not so fast mister."

He pouted and sat back. "Why not?"

I shrugged. "I feel like swimming."

As I pulled my shirt over my head Holden's eyes looked like they were going to bulge right out of his skull. His pupils dilated until it looked like they consumed his sight completely.

"What are you doing?" he asked after he was able to compose himself.

"Going swimming."

"Naked?! What if someone sees?"

I laughed, I had never skinny dipped but him being terrified made me feel even braver. I wanted to experience something with Holden for the first time. Too many firsts had already been wasted.

"Why, Holden. Are you saying you are too chicken? You are going to make me swim by myself?"

He laughed with a nervous grimace but stood up and began shedding his clothes. When we were undressed, I held his bare body against mine then pushed him back gently. I wiggled my fingers at him playfully and started walking to the edge.

"Whoa, whoa, whoa. I agreed to swim. I never agreed to jump off a cliff!"

"Holden, it's not even that high. Just look over the edge."

"No way!"

"Okay, then I'll meet you there."

I took two significant steps and threw myself off of the drop. I was in the air for breath then hit the water warmed from the sun. As I came up, I saw Holden fidgeting before taking a huge sigh and jumping. His arms flailing made me laugh and he hit the water about a foot from where I was. I swam over to where he surfaced.

"There!" he threw his arms up with a triumphant fist.

"You can't brag if you had to be talked into doing it."

"Oh yes, I can. I still did it."

I wrapped my arms around his neck, and he encircled me in his arms.

"I guess so."

"I think I deserve a reward."

I snorted but brought my lips back to his. As I followed him up a now familiar climb, we made our way to the shallower edge. I wrapped my legs around his waist, and when we came together, I was complete. This is what Holden did to me.

I heard songs that had never been played for me and tasted places I had never been. It didn't matter that we weren't each other's first when I looked at him. There was no room for comparing and were in synch with the matching of our heartbeats. I walked around all day thinking that I was a complete person on my own. But whenever we made love, I knew the truth. My heart and my body had been waiting for him, and the rest of the time I was walking around with my soul outside of my body.

*

"This is pretty empty as far as book collages go," Ash told me.

For every book I write, I like to make collages of images and passages that serve as a reminder of the tone of the book. It inspires me and keeps me on track when I start to drift away from my original vision.

Last year my collage was full of excerpts from the Tale of Two Cities, photos of lakes, characters profiles, and a drawing of Rusty, a little boy ghost that I had grown up with. The newest book I was working on, Strangers in the Shadows, was still a blank canvas. I had outlined parts of it but was stuck having a conversation with characters I wasn't able to fully hear yet.

After last year I was definitely holding back, afraid of what the voices might tell me. I wondered whether or not they were attached to real bodies. I had been able to move Rusty on, but I still felt stabs of guilt whenever I thought about him being stuck here for years alone while I ran away from my gift. He deserved much better than that.

"Yeah, it's not as easy as writing in college was," I told her.

"Do you have any ideas yet?" Ash asked, laying back on my bed and flipping through the Cosmo that was on my nightstand.

I let out a deep breath and looked at the notebook in front of me. "It's about a little girl who entertains herself by spying on her next-door neighbor. Her neighbor is beautiful and glamorous. She has a boyfriend, but maybe it's on and off again. Very dramatic. I feel like a death of some kind is coming up and I don't want to see it. I don't know if I am ready."

She sat up, giving me an arched eyebrow. "But the story is in your head? Just like Rusty's story was? That means it's probably a spirit that needs to reach out. If it's in your head, it's something you need to open yourself up to."

I wasn't worried about ghosts like Rusty, ghosts that ultimately wanted to move on. His mother Caroline was a different story. She had died a traumatic death and kept presenting herself to me still in her death state. She was such an angry spirit and destroyed the rooms she walked through. Goosebumps broke out on my arms, and I rubbed them absently.

"Do you remember how scary Caroline was? Sneaking up on me, screaming in ways I couldn't block out. It was awful, I was constantly walking on eggshells."

"Aren't you now? Except now you are choosing to ignore a child who might need you."

I sighed, the goosebumps softening as I saw the tic tac toe grin of Rusty once again. Seeing him move on was one of the most beautiful things I had ever witnessed. I never would have been able to see that light and genuinely appreciate it without experiencing the darkness first.

I shook my head. "Why do you have to be my conscience? This is scary. It's much easier if you just agree with me."

She snorted. "I'm your best friend. I don't have to agree with you. If you want to be babied, call Holden."

I laughed and smacked her leg. "Okay, okay."

"You'll try?"

I nodded. "I'll try."

I sat next to her and laid my notebook out on my lap. I lightly touched my wrist under my shirt sleeve where a scar was still raised from surgery last year. If I was sincere, it wasn't just the ghosts that I had been avoiding.

Lucas hadn't just run us down that night after Terry's award ceremony and stolen my mom from me. He had kidnapped Macy and me. Our house had a complete security makeover, but locks couldn't protect me in my dreams.

Trauma counseling had helped, but I felt like I had wrapped myself in bubble wrap the last month. I was dealing after the accident, but it was a work in progress. A fantastic week without thinking about it might be followed by a month straight of nightmares. I was finding my new normal. However, if I started this again, I was giving myself over to yet another terrifying situation. I didn't know how much more I could take before I lost myself to this helplessness completely.

*

"How's your homework coming along?" I asked Macy, who was set up at the dining room table with her computer and textbooks.

She gave me a dramatic sigh. "The first month of school should be easy, right? It's our last year, you know? But they must feel like they are running out of time because we just jumped right in."

I smiled and sat next to her, pulling out my manuscript and sitting down to force myself to outline. Maybe Macy's studying environment would help keep me focused. But more likely, she was the perfect person to procrastinate with.

She looked over at my notebook and shifted. "Terry told me that maybe I should start a journal. Where I could kind of talk to Mom and feel connected to her."

"Do you like that idea?"

"I think I should. Sometimes it's easy to pretend like Mom is still here, do you know what I mean? I can't see her or hold her, but I can hold onto things that she held onto. I have been keeping her magazines."

"Why?" I asked, even though it was way too easy for me to imagine. But it seemed like something she needed to talk about.

"Because she wanted them. I don't even read them; they are silly ones like Star. But they have her name on them. I don't want Terry to see them, so I keep them in a box under my bed."

"Does it make you feel better?"

"Sometimes."

"Then maybe a journal would be able to help you hold onto a piece of her."

"What if the things that I want to write about are upsetting?"

"Like what?" I asked.

Macy wrapped her arms around herself, and her gaze was glassy. "I hear you crying at night, too. Are you still dreaming about Lucas?"

I nodded with reluctance, not wanting to make her feel worse. She was already chewing on her lips, and her nails looked awful. Talking about everything was supposed to make it better, but sometimes it only reminded me of things that I had forgotten. The details faded only when I let them stay where they laid in my memory.

"I dream about him hurting Gina. The screams that came from you. I wake up with gunpowder in my nose. I keep thinking it's going to go away and then it doesn't. Terry doesn't get it."

"I know. But I do. And we will get through this together," I told her, fighting the urge to throw up.

24

I didn't want to think about Lucas either, but it wasn't something that you just got over. We had watched someone die, more than that, we had encouraged someone to kill another person. He was going to rape Gina, and in the beginning, I was almost proud of myself for helping her choose to protect herself. Then Terry came home and got that last vision from Gina, the one of her suffocating her mother.

Terry had called the police, hysterical. She told them that Gina had confessed to her. When the police arrested her, Gina was so caught off guard, she admitted it to the police. I remember Terry telling us what had actually happened. Gina had come from killing her mom to finding us with Lucas that day. I held the hand that was still fresh with scratches caused while Catherine fought to breathe and told her that she had the right to take another breath. It was disgusting, it was devastating.

Knowing what she had just done was impossible, but it didn't make what happened that night any easier to swallow. And it wasn't easy for Terry to forgive us, or for us to forgive ourselves.

"Other than that, the dreams, how are you?" I asked, needing to change the subject.

Macy sat back, crossing her arms over her chest. She seemed to be considering whether or not she wanted to get into whatever her latest drama was. If she was holding back, it had to be about Britney. She had been over almost every single day this summer and then her visits suddenly tapered off.

In the end, she didn't say anything at all.

Chapter 2

Terry

September 2015

Seeing pieces of my past life didn't feel like typical visions. It felt like walking through a doorway to get a glass of water and ending up in a house 300 miles away wearing a different body. It was abrupt and seamless in the same breath. Some pieces of this woman came to me in dreams or in flashes. Or, like right now, I fell into this past existence and sort of hung in the balance in my own life.

Our clothes make a trail to the end of my four-poster bed, a timeline of our passion. We go so long between meetings that often it feels like we won't make it to the mattress. Kerry breaks the buttons off of my shirts and has ripped more than one pair of slacks. My apartment always looks like a murder took place when it's time for him to go home.

"I hate when you leave like this," I told Kerry, holding his arm to keep him from getting out of bed as his cell phone rings in the pocket of his jeans.

I hadn't wanted a cell phone for this exact reason. They were huge and looked ridiculous. Kerry didn't jump every time my landline rang, cellphones were evil.

"And I hate it when you always make me feel guilty. You know I can't stay," he pulled away from me, and I watched the muscles in his forearms tense up.

I looked up at him, still blown away by his ink black hair and almost golden eyes. He was tall and often rested his chin

27

on the top of my head. I was safe in his arms. I was safe until I wasn't in his arms anymore and knew that he was with her instead.

I sighed, laying back on the pillows.

"I'm not trying to make you feel guilty. It's just hard not to think of how this makes me feel. I am the one who loves you. And you love me, there's no way it could be like this between us if it weren't meant to be. It doesn't make sense that you go back home to her when I am the one who needs you."

Kerry pulled on his jeans but crawled towards me. "How is it between us?"

There is a storm in his expressions that I have come to love. I wiggle down so that I am underneath him and pull him closer to me.

"It's amazing. Whenever you leave, all I can think of is the next time that you will be inside of me. It's the only time I feel like I am really alive."

He grinned and leaned down to trail a line of kisses from my collarbone to my jaw. I thought I had him back and began unbuttoning his jeans. Then his cell phone started ringing again. I wanted to throw the stupid brick out the window.

"B, I want to stay. You know I do. But I can't," he groans, pulling himself off and grabbing his shirt from the pile next to my vanity.

I bit my lip to keep myself from crying. It was the same story every week, and it ended the same way regardless of how upset it made me.

"Okay, fine. When will I see you again?"

Kerry sits to put on his shoes. "Wednesday? I have a couple of hours before work when Rachel has a doctor's appointment."

He froze as he realizes that he said her name. It's one of the rules. She doesn't belong in here, in my house. Not even her name.

"I'm sorry."

"I don't want just a couple of hours. It's been like this for months. I don't know why we don't just call it all off if this is all it's ever going to be."

Kerry crossed the room to sit next to me. "Stop. You don't mean that. Wednesday is all I have this week. But… I was going to wait to give this to you. "

He pulled a card from his back pocket and gave it to me. I opened it without expecting much, still not looking him in the eye. Inside the card was a piece of paper with directions to a hotel in Seattle, Kerry had scribbled a confirmation number underneath.

"You're going out of town?" I ask.

"No, we are going out of town. For your birthday. Let's take this weekend, figure out what the next step is."

I bite my lip and don't want to look at him. The next step? Does that mean he is finally ready to propose? To leave Rachel and be with me forever? It's been two years. I waited so long and tried to understand why it wasn't the right time. First, Rachel was finishing college and then her dad was sick. But it's been six months of nothing but waiting while she talked about planning a party for their five-year wedding anniversary.

He belonged to me. I was the one that he chose to spend New Year's Eve with and it was me he surprised at work on Valentine's Day. I was ready for this to be my whole life and not just the best, tiny sliver.

"Are you serious? That this is a big deal and that we are taking this next step together?" I ask, finally looking at him. I watch his body language closely.

He kissed my knuckles one by one and then stood up. "I'm serious. It's time."

I sigh, and it feels like two years' worth of breaths held. It seems like the turn of a new leaf, a new chapter, a new life. The world shakes from underneath me and pain spikes up to my knees.

"Ter?!"

I hear Macy's voice but have to claw my way back to my own consciousness. I feel cold condensation on my fingers, and my feet were wet. The sensation jerks me into myself. I see my sister in the kitchen doorway, looking concerned. She rushes over and grabs a dish towel.

"You are lucky this didn't break. What are you doing?" she asks.

I look down and realize that I had gotten a glass of water and tried to walk away, stuck in my old self. The self that was able to walk without help. My knees were trapped underneath me, and my muscles screamed in agony.

"Whoa, it's okay," Macy wrapped my arm around her and pulled me to my feet and over to the walker still sitting next to the kitchen sink.

"I'm all right, I just got a little light headed."

"Did it happen again?" Her eyes searched above my head, examining my aura with concern.

I nodded, unable to talk about it. She didn't know that the person I used to be had been in love with a married man. I didn't even know the whole story. But I already felt ashamed of her transgressions. Of sins that we now shared.

Reincarnation sounded foreign in my head, but was it any more farfetched then seeing the future? Was it crazier than seeing the past? I now knew that my soul had walked the earth before. And I also knew, without a doubt, that my soul had loved another more than life itself.

It wasn't just my past life's mistakes that I wasn't ready to share. It was also the sneaking suspicion that this part of me was essential to my future. My old soul was making a new appearance and seeking out another.

Kerry, or whoever Kerry's soul was these days, was here. His old soul lived inside of someone else walking the earth now. I knew that the love of my life, maybe of all of my existences, was out there somewhere. I knew I wanted to find them more than anything.   My sisters would never understand.

*

Dinner with CJ used to be my favorite part of the week. We took turns cooking, or rather, I cooked on my week, and he brought over take out when it was his turn. We spent hours at the table catching up even though we rarely let more than two days go between seeing each other again. He was with me every single day of my coma. Now I felt this vast distance between those days and now. Now Claire was here, insisting on cooking too and making herself a part of our routine. It was easy to see that Macy was reveling in it entirely, but I still wasn't sure if this was something that would last.

But then, Claire wasn't the only problem here. I was getting to know this new Claire just as I was getting to know whoever I had become when I woke up. I didn't quite fit into this life and was always a step behind.

"Will there be a book tour? I can't believe people can see your novel on shelves. It seemed like something you always talked about and now it's a reality," CJ was saying to Claire, passing her a carton of orange chicken.

"Tell me about it. It's still strange to me. I am not sure about a book tour yet. It's a tiny publishing house so I might have to garner a following before anything like that happens."

Claire looked at me carefully, noticing that I kept spacing out. I was proud of my sister, but something about this life seemed transparent now that my body was sharing two different existences. I knew what was going to happen here and it was too hard. I knew that I was terrified to work, that things were confusing with CJ, and that grieving my mom wasn't going to get easier. I didn't want to think about it anymore.

Thinking about Kerry and being kissed by him was a lot more appealing. I never felt lost or misunderstood when I became her, even for a few moments.

Macy breezed into the room, bringing her laughter with her. Britney trailed after her, her arm wrapped around her waist. They dropped their backpacks next to the kitchen door with a thump.

"Mm, Chinese," Macy leaned over CJ and stole a tray of egg rolls from the table. She headed downstairs with Britney, talking the entire time.

"I'm going to finish some editing. It was good to see you," Claire told us, nodding at CJ and following Macy downstairs.

With just the two of us at the table, the conversation quickly dried up. After finishing dinner, CJ helped me clear the table then stood by the back door, the awkwardness feeling like an extra person in the room.

"What are you up to tomorrow?" he asked me.

"I have some paperwork to catch up on. Taking a leave of absence requires a lot of signatures apparently. I need to transfer my clients to Stephanie at work."

I knew that he was waiting for me to ask him to stay. Whenever we had a free day, he slept here, and we talked until two in the morning. I loved waking up to him. But something had changed for him when I was hurt. He had finally made up his mind. I didn't know how long he would be okay with just talking until the early hours of the morning. How long he would be okay with us just being friends.

But he was CJ, and he wasn't going to put any pressure on me while I was still healing and adjusting. His resolve was solid though.

And I guess I needed to make my mind up as well because a part of me wanted to push him away so that whatever came next wasn't as hard. If I could change his mind, then I didn't have to feel so awful for wanting to belong to someone else.

"CJ, do you think it was my fault?" I asked.

He didn't have to ask what I was talking about. "No, Ter. Lucas is at fault for the accident. He was angry that you wanted to help Gina and he was losing control. And Gina is responsible for what happened afterwards with her mom and your sisters. She made the choices and knew that she was manipulating your family."

"What if I was distracted? That night we decided to go dancing, and I was trying to be carefree for the first time in months. I was singing along to the radio and making Claire laugh. But what if I had decided to go home instead? What if I had stayed alert? Maybe if I saw him following us, he wouldn't have been able to hit us like that. If we hadn't made plans, maybe my mom would still be alive."

CJ shoulders slumped, and I didn't have to know him well to see that he was hurt. I wasn't saying it, but I laid part of the blame on him as well. I was excited to be with him that night and not thinking clearly. Things might have been entirely different if he had just said goodnight.

"Do you really believe that?" he asked.

"I don't know. It's hard not to wonder what if."

"Your mom used to say that everyone's time was pretty much predetermined. Maybe that night ends differently in another version of our life, but I don't think that means that your mom would still be here today. Gina still would have killed Catherine and Lucas might have kidnapped you instead. What happened, happened. Placing the blame somewhere else is just going to make you crazy."

He tried to hold me, but I backed up against the wall.

"Will I see you next week? I'm beat," I looked down, shoving my hands in my pockets.

His bowed his head, but he forced the corners of his mouth up. "Sounds good. Sweet dreams."

When he let himself out, I sat back at the table, exhausted to my core. I loved CJ, I had loved him for most of my life. But right now, I just had no idea how to give him what he wanted. I had nothing left to offer that didn't feel like it belonged to someone else now. Maybe it had belonged to them all along.

*

If I slipped deep inside of my mom's covers, it sometimes feels like I can still sense her. I wanted to feel something that told me she was still here watching over me. Her room was the same, the same bedspread and angel knick-knacks on her nightstand. A single photograph being moved felt like enough to be unforgivable, I was glad my sisters had left it the way it was. Whenever I began to drown, I snuck in here and tried to communicate with my mom.

I quickly opened her closet and slid myself off of the walker to sit on the floor, breathing in the last very last wisps of her perfume leftover from the last time she got dressed. I ran my fingers over the cold tubes of her lipstick and looked at myself in her mirror. I held her photo albums on my lap and tried to conjure up the memories she saw when she put them together. I wanted to be able to get something from her by touching something she left behind, but so far nothing.

My sisters had the whole summer to come to grips with this new life and were beginning to heal. They didn't understand what I was going through. Even if we had experienced her death at the same time, they weren't best friends with Mom the same way that I was. They didn't know her favorite flowers were white roses and that she binge-watched reality TV. They didn't lose her the way I lost her.

If my mom were here, these broken pieces might fit back together. She would be the one going to physical therapy with me. Chatting with my therapist while she massaged my arms and cheering me on as I pulled myself out of that awful chair over and over. My mom would help me do my pelvis exercises at home without making me feel like I was trapped inside of myself. But she wasn't here, and life was becoming unbearable.

I missed her the most. How was it fair that I wasn't the one who was given the power to be able to communicate with her? Claire talked about being able to see her every once in a while, like it was the most casual thing in the world. Anger and resentment seeded itself in my chest every time she mentioned it. When side by side with forgiving them enough to be able to move on, hating her seemed like a natural choice.

Claire

September 2015

When I pulled into the driveway, I knew something was waiting for me. The hair on my arm stood up and dread twisted in the pit of my stomach. I took a lingering breath and tried to savor my night for a couple of moments before allowing the house to change how I felt.

It was a great night with Holden. He made us a midnight dinner, and we picnicked in the park next to his grocery store. The lake there had no memories attached to it but the new ones we were making. We traded bites of strawberries and dark chocolate, talking about our day and the future all at once. We kissed until the light started peeking through the night. When we were together entire nights slipped through our fingers in just minutes. It was 4:30 am, and I was just now getting home.

Taking a deep breath, I made my way to the front door. The air thickened as I made my way downstairs and sound just disappeared. I could hear my own breathing echoing in my head.

I remembered this wall of steam from when Rusty made his appearance back in my life and wondered if I had written a book about this ghost as well.

As I turned the corner, I saw a man lying on the ground. For one second the floor seemed to fall out from underneath me. It was Lucas, he wasn't dead. He had never been gone. My head felt light as I saw the way his blood had seeped out of his body and soaked into the carpet. The air was metallic and burned my nose. He was going to sit up any minute, the broken pieces of his body flapping as he crawled over to where I was standing. He had come back, and this time he wasn't going to stop until he killed me.

The image shook in front of me as the body on the floor shifted, and the light came in through the window. I wasn't in Gina's living room, I was home. The man sat up, and I realized he was barely a teenager.

He grinned, and his ankles crossed in front of him. His hair was sandy, and he had the most beautiful alabaster skin I had ever seen. I remembered wanting to kiss it, running my fingers through that hair and being wrapped in those arms. I remembered fearing and wanting him so much.

"Len?" I asked, stopping where I stood and staring at him.

He smirked and stretched, pleased with his surprise. It seemed like he knew that we would see each other again. When I was 13, he had disappeared, taking my first kiss along with him. It was hard to think about that part of my life; the edges of the memories were fuzzy. My parents had just divorced, and it was one bright spot. I stopped going to see him to be more like my dad, who had no gift.

I ended up missing him, but when I went back to the lake, he was gone. I was destroyed. I hated myself for being left behind. I was also relieved; I didn't have to carry around the secret of our days together anymore. He was the last ghost that I ever had an experience with and not having to tell him to go away saved me from a lot of pain. But now, it felt like no time had passed and we were picking up where we left off.

I should have been happy to see him after all of this time, but my senses heightened to the point of pain. I kept seeing Lucas on the floor, unmoving with blood creeping toward my shoes. I had to stare at Len without blinking to convince myself that he was the one in front of me, but my body still refused to come back down.

Len stood up and walked over to me. As he moved his essence seemed to flicker. I could glimpse pieces of color in the absence of him. He was attempting to appear serene, but his lips were pressed together tightly. His fists were balled. It had been a long wait for him.

"Hi," he reached over and grazed his fingertips against the inside of my forearms

I shuddered and pulled from him.

"Claire, are you okay?" he asked, his eyebrows furrowing.

"I'm just… shocked."

Len smiled, making my stomach flip-flop with nervousness I didn't understand.

"Why? I always knew that we would find our way back to each other."

I made no move to respond but was unable to pull away either. I was terrified to see him again. Would he hate me or blame me for how long he walked around alone? What if he felt like I disrespected his memory by not understanding where he went? What did he want from me? Did he even want to move on?

Because if he didn't want to move on, he wasn't going to allow me to say goodbye again.

*

"I can pay the cell phone bill now, and then we don't have to worry about it," I said to Terry.

I leaned over to grab my phone and open the account app.

Terry plucked the bill out of my hand. "You don't have to do that. It's not fair for you to have to pay for the weeks that you weren't using it."

I leaned back. Paying bills had become this push and pull with Terry. Her savings were being depleted and weren't being built back up because her bereavement pay hadn't gone through yet. Things were piling up because she wasn't letting me shoulder the burden regardless of how much I tried to push her.

"I don't mind Terry. I just got a royalty check. I can do this; it makes the most sense to pay off as many bills as possible while that money is in the bank. It's too easy to spend it when you don't have a goal in mind."

"What did you plan on spending it on before?" she asked, her expression blank.

"Before?"

"If you hadn't moved back in. If life had gone according to plan and you didn't have to worry about us."

My cheeks burned like she had slapped me. "But I did. And I do worry."

"Just tell me. What were your plans for that money?"

I took a deep breath, leaning away from her. I tried to picture a version of my life where this wasn't right in front of me, but it was harder than Terry wanted to believe. It wasn't possible to go back to the life I had before all of this. Given a choice, I chose my family. It wasn't as easy as deciding though, Terry was forcing me to fight my way back to them.

"I guess... Ash and I were planning on spending it on a deposit for an apartment. Other than that, I have no idea."

Terry stared at me. "Why that is not still the plan? You wanted to move in with Ash for a long time."

My mouth dropped open. "If you have something to say, just say it. I tried to understand because you are doing physical therapy and needed to work through your feelings, but your statute of limitations just ran out. I have been doing nothing but helping you, and you are shoving me away at every opportunity."

Terry cocked an eyebrow at me. "My statute of limitations ran out? Tell me, Claire, when can I stop being upset about the accident and the fact that Moms gone?"

"That's not even what I am talking about. I am talking about you and me. I am paying our bills, trying to pull my weight here, and you want nothing to do with it. What did I do wrong?"

Tears lined her cheeks, but her mouth was set in an angry line. "You left Claire. Over and over. I don't trust you. I don't want to rely on you because I know you will run away again."

I shook my head, pushing my own tears away. "No, I'm not going anywhere. I took care of Macy. I understand how much I hurt you guys and have tried apologizing a thousand times. I am sorry Terry! I am sorry. What can I do to make you trust me?!"

She put her head down on the table, hiding her face from me.

Slowly I got ahold of myself and was able to stop crying. Terry's shoulders were shaking, but I was not about to reach out to her and have her wretch herself away from me instead.

"Do you want me to move out? I don't want to. I want to make things better. But if you don't want me here... I understand," I choked out.

Terry was quiet for so long that I began to stand up. She straightened and tugged on the edge of my T-shirt.

"No, I want you here. It's what I always wanted."

44

"Then what? What is it going to take to make you feel like I belong here?"

She pulled me back into my seat.

"It's just that if you belong here, where do I belong? I used to be the one who took care of everyone. I kept everyone together. But now, my life is broken. You are the one running our household, and I don't know how to follow you."

I tried to nod. I had never wanted this kind of leadership or responsibility. It was hard to swallow, but I was doing it. I needed her to support me and tell me I was doing a good job. All I wanted in the world was to make my big sister proud. If she hated me for leading, then this bitterness would poison us forever. There was no room for anything else, especially love.

"Just give me some time," she whispered into my shoulder, hugging me.

I hugged her back. Then, I looked her in the eye and grabbed the cell phone bill off the table.

"Okay, you have time. But you need to let me take care of us, or there will be nothing left."

A glare flitted over Terry's features. This wasn't over. She didn't want to let go of her idea of control, and she definitely didn't want to share it with me.

She was terrible, and for the first time since Terry came home, I realize that she knew it. She was hard on me for a reason. I sank into my chair, meeting her gaze firmly. She stared back and let the moment draw out. As I memorize the curve of her nose and the closeness of her beautiful green eyes, I thought of Princess Bride.

It has been my sister's favorite movie since we were young. I have been able to quote the entire thing since I was 9 because she watched it at least once a week. Towards the end, Prince Humperdinck challenged Wesley to a fight to the death. Wesley told him that instead, they would fight to the pain. That he would chop him into pieces and leave him so terrible that he would make kids cry until the end of his days. The idea of that terrified me when I was younger, it was the worst punishment I could think of.

Until now. Because this was our fight to the pain. I was horrible to my mother and sisters while we were kids. I pushed them away and said hurtful things that I am sure they will never be able to forget. Terry took care of me and was easy on me because she was the big sister and I was just a kid.

But I wasn't a kid anymore. I had been begging her to let me help her raise Macy and be her equal. Here was the initiation.

I had to take all of her raw pain and bear it just like she was forced to do for all of these years. Facing her hurt was the only way to make it to the other side. She wanted to tear me down until I was a different person because growing up was always painful. Change always hurt a little bit, sometimes a lot. It had to.

This was Terrys fight to the pain. If I gave up now, there were no second chances. So, I stared back at her, letting her make me uncomfortable. Finally, recognition dawned on her face. She laughed a little and relaxed.

*

The grass pokes into her bare side, but she knows that complaining will just make him mad. If she tried to stay quiet, he finished more quickly. Sometimes she was able to just sort of float away. She focused on how nice it was kissing him.

But she wished it didn't go any further than that. She concentrated on him telling her that she was beautiful and ignored how those words needed repayment. He held her close, her shirt already off and looking forlorn next to her shoes. His breath was thick on her back as he inched forward and rubbed his fingers along her thigh before finding his way under her skirt.

I sat up gasping, running my arms down my body to rid myself of the last remnants of the dream. I had promised Ash that I would open myself up to the ghosts of the house and contact whatever child was calling to me. But so far, all that I seemed to absorb was terrible pain and confusion.

All of the dreams followed the same pattern, a little girl feeling frozen in her body as someone she trusted touched her. Panting in her ear, his breath sweaty and heavy on her neck. I dreamt of her wanting to cringe and forcing her mind away from what was happening. She wants to scream, but there was no strength left in her. She floated away, pretending she is anywhere but there.

I take a deep breath, focusing on the dream so that I could pinpoint any details that might help whoever I was supposed to meet. A huge part of me wanted to build a wall around these memories so that they couldn't touch me anymore, to distance myself far away from what that felt like. But part of this gift was being brave, so brave that lost spirits can rely on my strength to set them free.

"If you are still here, it's okay. You are safe. Talk to me, let me help you," I whisper into the room.

After waiting a moment, I sat up and threw my legs over the side of the bed. I wanted to be this home to be a safe place for spirits. But these dreams made me want to scrub the regret and shame off my own body.

Chapter 3

Claire

September 2015

Missy had been my mom's best friend since I was in elementary school, which is probably why I have been avoiding her. Actually, I avoided her a lot while I was growing up as well. Missy saw right through a person's bull and confronted you if she thought you were dishonest. She was loud and over the top, and she was an empath.

Her gifts were never as strong as my mom's, but she was the sole person outside of our family that was open about being psychic. The last time we spoke was at my mother's funeral. She had called a few times, but it was too painful to face her grief along with my own. When my mom told me that I needed her help to contact a spirit guide, I wanted to make a million excuses.

But I had made excuses to my mom for long enough. I looked her up in my mom's date book and called before I could second guess myself. She was surprised but free that afternoon. We were now sitting cross-legged in the living room attempting to meditate.

"Meditation has not been super successful for me," I said quietly, cracking open an eye to look at her.

She was short with freckles sprinkled over her nose and cheeks and always seemed to be wearing gold bangles on her wrist. Her and my mom looked so much alike that it hurt my heart to be in the same room as her. When she laughed, and I heard my moms tinkling along with hers. I imagined them sitting at the dining room table sharing a bottle of wine. It was like she was still here.

"I miss her too. But stop, we need to focus. I am here because she knows I can help you. It's not easy for me either," Missy said, locking eyes with me.

I blushed, but she just held my cheek for a moment and then went back to her meditation.

After about a half hour of silence, she sat back and nodded to me like she was ready to talk.

"What does a spiritual guide do exactly? Besides helping me set up boundaries," I ask, letting myself fall back as well.

"They help you strengthen your gift. Whatever you need, spirit guides help you accomplish it. Enhancing your meditation focus, helping you locate particular ghosts, keeping out ghosts that shouldn't be contacting you, and sorting pure spirits from the dangerous ones. You might not always be able to tell if a ghost is giving you their true face."

"Dangerous ones?"

She winced as if remembering something unpleasant. "Not every spirit out there is human...anymore. You have experienced the shadow figures?"

50

I nodded, my arms breaking out into goosebumps like I had dipped them in ice water.

"I know that a lot of people think they were never human, but I disagree. I believe they are spirits left in the in-between for too long. Shadow figures prey on youthful energy to become stronger. They target weak people and spirits and steal their humanity. Then the spirits become less human and more shadow. Does that make sense?"

I think about how dark Rusty was becoming and how afraid he was of the darkness. His cheeks were pale and highlighted the bruises under his lashes from a lack of sleep. Anger had changed his essence completely. Once we started searching for his mother together, his color had improved, and his smile became as dazzling as it had been when we used to play together.

"I think I have witnessed the beginning of a spirit fighting that change."

Missy leaned forward and touched my shoulder. "And you moved them on? That won't make the shadow figures here very happy. If they see you as a threat, they will try to make sure you are helpless."

My stomach twisted, and my head swam lightly.

After promising to keep practicing, I hugged Missy goodbye and then headed to our enclosed patio to read in the afternoon sunlight.

As I turned the corner, I saw a beautiful lady sitting on one of the loungers. She looked to be about 30 and had an air of confidence. Her thick brown hair was draped over her shoulders, and her brown eyes seemed very familiar. When she grinned at me, I realized that it was the same face that had peeked over my backyard fence throughout my childhood. Back then I thought she was a neighbor, but of course not. She was my first ghost. How many neighbors walked around with blood on their clothes? The red dots decorated her shirt and paints in spurts.

"Barbara?" I asked.

Speaking her name seemed to give her power, and she solidified even more. Chills went through me. I had just outlined my new book featuring a mysterious neighbor that has to help the young heroine confront her fears. The night before I had been excited to delve into that character and learn more. But now I felt like I had been caught going through her underwear drawer.

"Claire, you've grown up beautifully."

I sat across from her, unsure where to begin.

"Are you here for me? Do you need help?"

She shook her head. "I am here for you. I think that you are the one who needs help. Your mom sent me, she told me that you needed a spirit guide. I feel like I have spent so much time protecting you already, it was a natural decision."

I nodded, feeling a kinship with her I wasn't able to explain.

"You spoke to my mom?"

Barbara beamed at me, and I was filled with peace and calm.

"Protecting you now is more important than ever."

"Why?" I looked around as if the dangers were hidden behind the cabinet.

"A huge change in your life, in all of your lives. It's going to rock the energy in this house irrevocably. It will focus itself on you, and you might not be able to rely on your sisters."

"What?"

Her words brought to light so much fear, fear that I would never be able to shed. I had spent the last half a year striving to fit in and wondered if I would ever be close to Terry and Macy again. But no, I guess it wasn't meant to be. My heart clenched and breathing became harder.

"Rely on them how?"

Barbara smirked but then tried to recover. "My alliance is with you. I see your future and your path. They don't always have the same priorities as you."

Yet, it was more than that. It wasn't just the priorities. It was Barbara telling me that I might have happiness ahead of me, but it might come at the cost of my relationship with them.

*

I'm going to die, here and now. Terry had been keeping to herself since our argument, which means I had been cooking and eating by myself. I don't mind eating a meal alone. I usually grab a book and read it while enjoying whatever I have put together. It's the putting something together part that's causing a problem. I still cannot cook for the life of me, and just the idea of making something other than a bowl of cereal sent my stomach rolling.

It would be easy to ask Terry to make dinner tonight or even just a grilled cheese sandwich for me so that I didn't starve. But that meant admitting that I somehow gave myself food poisoning. Also, asking her to cook for me when it was something that she insisted on doing regardless of how much pain she was in just made me feel worse. She didn't want to trade off days cooking, but I saw the way the spatula shook and the way she curved her back inward.

I gave up looking through our cupboards for something foolproof and decided to go lay down in my room instead. I flopped down on my rumpled comforter and buried my head in pillows that still smelled like Holden's last sleepover. As I rolled over, I gave a little shriek. Len was crouched next to the bed with his nose inches from mine.

"Len! Could you knock or something? Just because you don't have to make noise doesn't mean you shouldn't."

He grinned. "I can knock. But startling you was just as cute as I imagined."

I sat up with care to keep my stomach from churning. It wasn't just the food these days. Every time I saw Len, I found myself being pulled to him a way that was out of my control. When I was in middle school, I considered him the most attractive guy I had ever met in real life.

He became my confidant and made me feel like a priority when I was the most lost in the world. It was hard not to feel like we had just picked up where we left off, like I still belonged to him and was somehow always 13.

At the same time, there was this vast blankness around the time that we were together. I had chalked it up to the divorce and wanting to block out the worst of it. But, was that it? Did something happen between us that my subconscious wanted to hide from me? Did I just stop showing up or was it something worse? I wished I remembered more but didn't want to ask him what I was missing. If it was terrible, it might push him away.

As if reading my mind, Len gave me a sly leer and sat next to me.

"Do you remember our days by the lake?"

I sat straighter, almost startled. Those days were some of my most intimate memories of my early teen years. Len had been my first kiss, a kiss I counted before anyone else.

"I do," I answered, blushing like I was still wearing that Barbie T-shirt he had once teased me for.

"That time… I was kissing your neck and touched your breast. It was the first time you had ever been touched like that. And you made this noise," he was leaning in, his forehead almost resting on my shoulder.

A shiver ran through me as the memory came to me. I remembered the sound. Of shock. I didn't want him to do it, but I didn't ask him to stop either. I turned my head away from him and saw a photo of Holden and me from Labor Day. I moved away from him and tried to change the subject.

"Where do you go when you're not here?" I asked.

He rubbed his neck and looked away. "I kind of go away… I used to be at the lake because... I was confused, and my body was still there. And you came to see me. But then I sort of lived because you thought I should and I got stronger because of that. But then you left. And I drifted away."

I looked down. It was never easy to hear that I had left someone behind, but it was an accusation that I kept having to face over and over.

"And then?"

Len trapped me with his pit less pupils until I had to break the gaze. I was beginning to realize that I might not want to know where lost spirits roamed.

"There's a middle place. It looks like this house, this world, but everything is draped in a thick mist that's hard to see through. It's easy to give yourself to the fog, but then it becomes darkness. And the shadows come after you."

I rubbed my arms like I was cold but the only chill in the air was inside of me. Missy's warning rang in my ears, and I wondered if I was beginning to lose Len the same way that Rusty had started to let go.

"Len, I know it's easy to give in. But don't let yourself go there anymore. Stay here with me. I can help you. What do you need to move on? To be free?"

Even as I extended my help, I wanted him to leave. I worried about leading him on when he was still stuck in what we used to be to each other. I couldn't be with him, but I wanted to be his friend and help him get through this.

"I don't need anything. All I ever wanted was to stay here with you."

"Then stay until we figure out what to do," I said, leaning forward and grabbing his arm.

As my skin covered him, I was surprised to find it cold and stable. He clenched his teeth, and he became smoke again.

"You left. And they came after me."

"I'm not going to leave again. Why won't you trust me?" I asked.

"Because you will leave again. Just like Caroline."

"Caroline? What the hell does she have to do with this? She is gone, I made sure of that."

Len shook his head. "Not now. Then. She tricked my dad into loving her, and she ruined our family, her and that baby.

You are just like her; you ruined my life and are going to leave me behind to clean up the mess."

I shook my head at him, exasperated.

"How can you know that? I want to make things better."

Len stood up and gave me a once over, his eyes settling on my abdomen.

"Claire, you will leave. You're going to have a baby."

*

The smell of the antiseptic mixing with the burritos in the hot deli tray made my head swim. Locking the gas station bathroom door hadn't done anything to make me feel like I had any semblance of privacy, but it was better than being at home. I had no idea what was going to happen in the next three minutes, and I didn't want to have to yell at my sisters through the bathroom door or try to hide the pregnancy test packaging in the trash.

I put the test on the counter and set my phone for three minutes. I took breath after breath, wanting to steady myself but making myself sick in the process. I heard a tiny scratching noise and looked around in a panic, expecting a rat hiding behind the industrially sized paper towels on the floor. I was alone, but my body broke out in goosebumps, and I realized I wasn't sensing this state of reality anymore.

I still had the door shut but saw the middle-aged man sitting on the other side of it nonetheless. He scratched at the door, crying and holding his ribs. Blood spilled between his fingers, the hot pulsation of the gunshot wound that spiraled through his ribcage and nicked his lungs. A month ago, he had been shot while closing up the gas station. He had died on the way to the hospital but lost consciousness while still laying on the dirty tile of this Conoco.

He was confused and thought I was there to help him.

"You're gone, you were shot," I tried to whisper without the very alive replacement cashier hearing me from the counter.

The man moaned and began hitting the door with weak smacks, struggling with the knob.

"Go away, please. Find your light and give up your pain," I whispered in a frantic voice, leaning down to the doorknob and projecting my voice through the crack in the door.

"Miss? Are you alright in there?" A slight bang shook the door, and I jumped back, gasping.

I grabbed the test off the counter with some paper towel and shoved it in my sweatshirt pocket. I eased the door open and saw the cashier, a young girl popping Juicy fruit with a bored look.

"Are you okay? I thought I heard crying."

I shook my head. "Just fine. Thanks."

Pushing past her, I took a massive breath of fresh air before sitting in my car to bawl. The man was gone, but he must still be locked there, scared and lost in his pain. I went to my pocket to get my keys and grabbed the forgotten test instead. With shaking hands, I unwrapped it, and my life changed. It was positive.

Terry

September 2015

"Hey, what's up?" I asked Holden, holding the front door open for him since his arms were full of flowers.

"Nothing much. Tomorrow is my and Claire's 3-month anniversary. I have to work but I wanted her to come home to something beautiful."

I smiled at him, there were so few guys out there as sweet as Holden. I hoped Claire knew how lucky she was.

"She's out buying paper for her printer with Ash, but come in and wait. I was just about to make some coffee."

He brightened. "Peppermint mochas?"

I beamed back at him; girly coffee was our shared vice. Holden loved spiced chai lattes and Frappuccino's but refused to order it in person whenever we went to Starbucks. When he stole yet another of my mint mochas, I learned to make them at home so that he could enjoy them in private.

"Of course."

He followed me into the kitchen and went under the sink for a vase to put the flowers in.

"How's it going? What is Mac up to?" Holden asked, sitting at the little kitchen table.

I sighed. "She's at Britney's. They are going to a party tonight, and she is super excited about attempting her aura matchmaking for the first time. She thinks that she has cracked the code and is setting up two of her friends from school based on the auras."

"How does she know they are compatible?"

"She told me that she just has a feeling and that trial and error makes the most sense."

Holden laughed. "But they are her friends? That doesn't seem like a good idea. If they have a bad break up, they might blame her for introducing them to each other. Trial and error doesn't really work when its two actual people."

I snorted and grinned at him. I had just said the same thing to Claire. Ever since the accident, Claire had been treating Macy like she was made of papier mache. I understood it, but she still needed guidance, especially when it came to our gifts. Love wasn't as easy as mixing two colors together. Shaking my head, I stirred half and half in a saucepan along with semi-sweet chocolate and peppermint extract.

"It's not just the possibility of causing issues with her friends that I am worried about. She is playing with her gift when she isn't done fully developing it yet. I don't want her to be disappointed or start telling people about it. Even if they do believe her, they might want her to set them up and then blame her if it doesn't work out. She still needs to protect herself."

Holden nodded slowly. "It's hard not to worry about them. They worry about you too."

I turned, putting a cup of finished of mint coffee goodness in front of him. I wondered if Claire had told him about the past memories and the visions. Probably not, she kept things pretty close to the vest. But Holden did seem to bring out more trust in her than I ever thought possible.

"Maybe I need it. We all sometimes do."

He took a huge drink, breathing like a dragon when he realized it was still steaming. "How is physical therapy going?"

I sat back and shook my head. "It's hard. I never realized how hard pulling yourself out of a chair is."

My days were full of this kind of crap lately. Physical therapy, trips to the neurologist to test my motor functions, the pharmacy, and the pool for low impact exercise. I couldn't even remember what it was like to be able to meet a friend for lunch at the drop of a hat. The fact that Claire and Macy had come out of this whole thing unscathed made it even harder. They were able to live out their lives without any worries.

"It won't always be like this," Holden told me, leaning forward and squeezing my shoulder.

Over the last month, Holden seemed to be here for me more than anyone else. He had come into our life so suddenly and fit like he had been a part of the design from the beginning. He made it feel like life wouldn't always be hard and complicated. Perhaps we would just keep adding people like Holden to our family until it felt so full that we didn't notice the holes anymore.

*

I can smell the lake water on my hair, and it's as easy as closing my eyes and falling into her, into myself.

"I'm going to be late for work… again," Kerry says, still burying his face in my breasts.

I ignore him, nibbling on his shoulder and spreading our blanket further with my feet.

We are in my favorite place in the world, the lake where we had our first date. It feels like a million years ago. Kerry was sure, and I was so reserved. He had packed a box of chocolates, and I laughed at him, telling him I hated chocolate. He never forgot to bring my Skittles whenever we met, a homage to that first meeting. It always made me feel like he knew me better than anyone.

He cradled my neck, his fingers digging into my skin, but I didn't mind. With a deep breath, he pulled himself away.

I pushed myself up onto my elbows.

"You're actually leaving?" I asked.

Kerry looked over his shoulder, registering my still naked chest and then forced himself to look away.

"Please get dressed, this is hard enough."

I laughed. "I noticed."

He blushed despite our history.

I laid back. "Maybe I'll stay. Maybe I'll take a naked nap then have a late lunch at Zips."

His shoulders slumped. Zips was a low blow. He really could not resist their hamburgers. After one of our trysts, it was our favorite place to go for a late-night snack. We talked for hours, him devouring a giant bacon cheeseburger and me eating my weight in fries.

"Mm," I stretched out, rolling over and tilting my head back to expose my collarbone. I arched my back and massaged my neck.

In a second Kerry was back, his shirt off and his skin hot against mine.

"You're impossible."

I felt the keyboard under my fingers and was returning to myself regardless of how hard I fought to stay there in Kerry's embrace. My skin was sunburned, and I tasted milkshake at the back of my throat.

I took a deep breath, grounding myself. He was here. Maybe not in Spokane, but he was here in this time. As my head cleared, I found myself typing a name into my browser. Eli Garth. I had no idea what to expect, but when a Facebook profile popped up, I knew it was him from the first glance. I pulled it up on my screen, holding my breath.

He looks completely different, but I was sure I did as well. Kerry had the same ink-black hair, but his eyes were the color of honey. Eli didn't look like Kerry, but he made me feel exactly the same way. He has dark blue eyes and shaggy black hair, and a Savage Garden T-shirt was hanging from his slight frame. It's him. My heart fluttered, and I forced myself to take a breath.

He lived in California and seemed to work as a welder. I clicked on the pictures, wanting to devour each one. I felt like I knew him, so it's strange to discover facts that caught me off guard. When I saw a beautiful blonde girl in the seventh picture, my stomach recoiled. She was gorgeous, and from the way he is hugging her, it's clear she isn't a family member. I click on the photo and a tag pops up, Kristy Baker. I go back to Elis profile page and see that he is in a relationship with her.

Black spots dance in my vision and I clenched my hands so hard that my nails cut into my palms. Kristy is curvy and beautiful, perfect in every way. I looked down at myself in scrubby pajamas. Even dressed in my best jeans and a T-shirt, I didn't hold a candle to her.

Would our past shared history be enough to make him look beyond how different I was from Kristy? Would he be able to see the real beauty in me? I didn't want to have to compete with her but placing blame on him made even less sense.

Of course, it's normal that he's in a relationship. A part of me feels guilty for feeling the way that I have about CJ for my whole life because once I knew that Eli was out there, it all just seems... empty.

But thinking of my life with CJ as empty sends me into a spiral of guilt. How could I wonder what else was out there? How could I be contemplating deserting him after he took such good care of me? Yet, I wouldn't be able to really give him my whole heart if I wasn't sure that he was right for me.

I pause with my mouse over the friend request button. Why am I hesitating? I knew from the moment I remembered my past life that it was so that I had a way back to him. But reaching out changes my life forever. Deciding to pursue him will separate my life into before and after. At the same time, what other choice did I have? I pressed the button and chewed on my already ragged bottom lip. Now I am just waiting for the after.

Chapter 4

I wasn't trying to ignore Holden. But I also wasn't ready to talk yet. I wanted to process my feelings in private and figure out what to do, which was impossible when you lived with two sisters. As I sent another phone call to voicemail, they shared a look.

I was getting tired of it, but I wasn't ready to tell them either. Holden tried hard to connect the last time we hung out. He saw that I was overwhelmed and wanted to help me so much. But letting him hold me might dissolve my reservations entirely and I wasn't sure I wanted that yet.

I was emotionally exhausted from thinking about this pregnancy constantly. What if he wanted to make love? Were the changes in my body already noticeable? What about going through the rouse of protection when I knew it didn't matter anymore?

I didn't want him to know yet because I wasn't sure how I felt. Abortion was entirely out of the question, but that didn't mean I was ready to raise a child. What about my writing career? What about Holden's future? What about our relationship? I didn't want a shared child to be something that pushed us apart or made us commit to each other for the wrong reasons. Being responsible for someone's entire future was more significant than just the two of us. We might ruin this little persons life.

All of the articles I had binged throughout the last week told me that the baby was barely the size of a poppy seed, microscopic by all accounts. However, the situation didn't feel microscopic.

This was my future and the future of my relationship with Holden. I wanted it and hated the circumstances all at the same time. It's too much, I broke out into a cold sweat whenever I thought about it. I wanted to avoid it, but my sisters didn't seem as keen to let my bizarre behavior go.

"Did you and Holden get into a fight?" Macy asked as I turned my phone to silent.

"Not really. I just have a lot on my mind right now," I pretended to be absorbed in the manuscript in front of me.

"He's going to think something is wrong. Just answer and tell him you will call him later," Terry says.

I glared at her. "Maybe I don't want to talk to him later."

Her cheeks reddened, and she glared back at me. "Wow. If you need a tampon Claire, don't hesitate to ask."

I blushed deeply. "Sorry. I'm just having an off day."

Macy's eyes darted around my head, narrowing and widening until she looked like they were going to pop out of her head.

"What are you doing?" I asked.

"What the hell is up with your aura? It's always been so green and consistent. It almost looks like you have a layer of gold mixed in. It's really crazy. You have a light show all around you."

I sat up stiffly and flailed my arms around as if I could flick the colors away. "Knock it off! Stay out of my aura."

Macy pinned me with her gaze. "Claire. Why do you have two auras?"

Terry's mouth dropped open a little bit, and she looked around my head like she was trying to see the auras as well.

"I… how can you even tell? Maybe you need to practice."

Macy tried to huff playfully, but it was apparent I hurt her feelings by blaming it on her gift. I sighed, not wanting to piss her off on top of everything else.

"I'm sorry. You're not… wrong," I told her.

"Claire, are you pregnant?" Terry asked, coming to sit closer to me.

I thought of the million pregnancy tests I took and gently took my sister's hand, letting her in. I showed her the scene at the gas station. I refused to believe that first test and ended up buying six more and taking them in the middle of the night. I ripped them open and almost broke a few. I watched the pink positives line up on the counter and then put them in a Ziploc bag to hide in my dresser.

I was filling a box under my bed with magazines from the doctor's office, feeling voracious for information. When the baby's ears grew and when movement usually happened. I shared my elation and fear. Terry's eyes were misty as she leaned in towards me.

"Claire!" Macy shrieked, sitting on my other side to share the vision.

Warmth rushed through me, and I was aware of Terry sharing the memories with Macy. Macy didn't even reach this time, and despite the circumstances, it was terrific to be at the center of this shared power. It was so pure and helped me feel strong.

"Don't be happy yet… because I can't be happy yet. What if this… ruins what we have? What if Holden isn't happy? What if I can't take care of them? What if I am the worst thing that happened to this baby?" I ask, finally saying the word out loud broke the last of my reservations, and I burst out crying.

Terry and Macy both leaned forward to wrap me in their arms.

"Impossible. Holden is not that guy, and it's irrelevant because we are here for you. Whatever you decide, we are behind you. We will figure this out together," Macy said.

I nodded, wanting to believe her. But the last couple of months I hadn't felt like part of them. I have felt like an outsider watching Terry and Macy continue to bond and knew that it might never be the same for us. On top of all of that, money was beginning to get tight. I had saved as much of my royalty checks as possible, but Terry's insurance ran out in November, and I didn't know how much physical therapy she still needed.

Her walking was getting much better, but it wasn't possible to put a deadline on recovery. I worried about being able to afford it all without her working. It wouldn't just be the extra sessions and medication that she needed.

Soon I would need my own battery of doctor visits and eventually bottles, diapers, and a complete nursery. Would the issue of bills become so stressful that it broke us apart completely? What if a baby made it worse? What if they blamed me for needing them when I never cared if they needed me? What if this is my punishment?

Thinking of this baby as a punishment sent me spiraling into guilt as well. I was already connected to them and wanted them more than I could even put into words. But it was all tangled with all of the things that I was afraid of.

As Terry's squeezed my bare shoulder, a vision seeped in through my skin. The last time she had shared a vision with me, she was pissed and filled me with pictures of my mom crying alone on the kitchen floor. I was sick for weeks afterward.

Terry must not have realized she was sharing again, and I hated that I made her feel this way. She was frustrated, picturing me setting up a crib in Ash's bedroom. Laughing with her and putting together a rocking chair. I tasted her anger and confusion.

Why did she immediately think that I didn't want to raise my child here? Why did she assume I wanted Ash more than I needed my sisters? Did she even want part of this at all? Did she think this was a mistake?

*

Getting to know Barbara should have been seamless for me. My mom sent her to me, which meant that she thought she was right for my spiritual journey. But Barbara honestly wasn't making it any easier for me to meditate.

I needed to learn to put up walls between me and the spirit world so that ghosts weren't able to approach me whenever they wanted to. Now that I was sharing my body… it was even more necessary. However, the more I tried to focus the more my mind pulled in a million different directions.

I sighed and began meditation for the 43rd time in the past hour, closing my eyes. Almost immediately I saw dirty gray hands jerking in spastic shakes, pulling themselves closer to me, throwing open the sunroom door and reaching for my ankle. Instead of my living room, I was surrounded by thick gauzy smoke with porous concrete beneath me. Distorted bodies dragged themselves over the wasteland, swarming to wherever they smelled blood.

These weren't the shadow figures that I was accustomed to. The figures of pure darkness that were solid and wispy at the same time. These creatures were gray and seemed to be made up of frenzied dust and gangly limbs that moved in seizures. Their skin stretched over their bones to the point of transparency, and their mouths were pits of black that looked endless. I didn't know what they were, but I knew that they were starving.

I tried to visualize bricks, one by one separating them from me. But I wasn't fast enough, and they slithered over my wall. Bricks fell in their wake, their crepey fingers closed around my calf. I opened my mind's eye and caught the eye of the creature in front of me. Its eyes were moving in crazy circles then suddenly caught mine. I saw the openness of their midnight pupils. They held me, and slowly the creature climbed my body, scratching at my waist.

"No!" I screamed, opening my eyes and breaking the connection.

I was sweating and brushed my legs where the halfing had caressed me.

Barbara sighed. "That wasn't great. You still aren't trusting me fully."

"Trusting you? Where were you? Every time I meditate and open myself up, all I see are those disgusting creatures. I don't see you anywhere. I thought you were supposed to be protecting me. Teaching me!"

74

She sat back. "I am teaching you. But I can't protect you unless you trust me. Unless you trust me with your soul and your gift."

I took multiple deep breaths, settling the deep shaking inside of myself. I worried that those half monsters had gotten inside of me and were exploring my organs. I felt them root out my abdomen where a child grew quietly.

"What do they want? They seem different than the shadow figures."

"No, they are the same. Here they seem like shadows because people have a hard time coming to grips with their true form. But there, in the half world, they are as gray as dust. And they are so hungry and bold. In that place, they can get what they want much easier."

"What do they want?" I repeated.

I searched her brown irises for an answer. Her face was familiar to me, but she was nothing more than a stranger. I wanted to trust Barbara and feel calm when I was with her, but I wasn't there yet.

It felt like the worst time to try to get to know her, even if she could be an important person in my journey. A spirit guide needed to be someone I went to when I was afraid. But right now, I was more scared for my child than anything else, which she didn't seem to think was very important.

She looked at me, almost bored. Since finding out about my pregnancy, she had seemed very impatient. I knew that she wanted to keep me safe and I was more focused on figuring out my future than meditation. But I was beginning to realize that reflection might be necessary to me having a future in the first place.

"They want the spirit inside of you. New life is delicious for someone who has been without breath for so long. If they are able to turn that spirit black, they are reborn in a way as well. They will kill the child in an attempt to control it."

My stomach rolled into it, choking me and forcing bile into my throat.

"It's that easy? They can just take them? Change them into something else?"

Barbara gave me what I supposed she thought was a supportive look, but her face was twisted into a grimace instead.

"Of course not. They need your permission."

*

"Are you mad at Holden? Len asked, startling me.

I looked down at my bare feet and the sandals next to them. When Len had shown up in my yard while I was pulling up dry weeds, Holden had arrived at the same time. I was overwhelmed, and when Len asked to take a walk with me, I agreed. I left my house behind just as Holden rang the doorbell.

"I'm not avoiding him. I just… I don't know what to say. This is easier," I said.

Len smiled, and for a moment I remembered how attractive I once thought he was. "I'm not saying I mind, but what makes it easier? We haven't seen each other in years. We are ancient history."

I watched him, closer than I really wanted to be. Something about how he was enjoying me being here with him instead made my insides twist with anxiousness.

"Aren't we?" he asked, attempting to hold my hand.

"Of course," I said, taking my hand back and resisting the urge to wipe it off on my jeans.

Being around Len filled me with so much confusion. A very young part of me was drawn to him like I was still a teenager figuring out who I was. But there was something else more profound that felt very much like fear.

"You know, you don't need him," Len said, sitting next to me.

"For what?"

"To raise the baby. You don't need him. I know why you are scared. You talked about it a lot when we were growing up. Having kids ruined your parent's relationship."

I sat up and tried to move away from him. I wasn't ready to grapple with that reality. I didn't remember saying that, but it was too close to home to discount entirely. I had looked at my mom's family albums enough to notice the difference.

Before us, they were crazy in love. They had fun together and looked at each other in a way that every girl dreams of. Once we joined them in the photos, they pulled further and further away from each other. I didn't want to bring a child into this world and then make them feel like they were the reason their family fell apart.

"I don't know what to do," I said, sweating even thinking about it.

"Stay with me. It's the one way to protect them from heartbreak."

I wanted that to feel comforting, but his offer just made me more scared. Len wasn't really here. He wasn't a part of this world enough to have an effect on my life at all. He was just another person that I had let down.

The grin seemed glued in place, but I saw him flicker in a way that scared me. For a second the air next to me was empty, and then he was back.

"Len… Are you fading away?" I whispered.

"I think so," he said, rubbing the back of his neck.

"Why now?"

He looked down and fiddled with a frayed thread on his sleeve. "Don't you see them?"

As he spoke, I saw him flicker again, and at that moment I also saw the hundreds of shadowy figures standing around us in a circle. They seemed to draw closer to us then lean back again. I reached out and touched his cheek. He was made of a freezing smoke that was almost solid. His humanity was draining away, and I had no idea how to save him. Being his friend seemed like a flimsy promise.

"I'm going to keep you safe," I said stiffly, choking back tears, feeling the crush of guilt once again.

I meant it. I was going to save Len, and I was going to save this baby. If I didn't, he became one the ones that I was learning to fight. I didn't know if I was capable of resisting an eternal face that looked like someone I had loved. Something told me that I should be more afraid of that than anything else.

Terry

October 2015

"What are you looking for?" I asked Macy, wiping the sleep from my eyes and going to the cupboard for a coffee mug.

She looked like she was still wearing her makeup from the night before and was furiously looking through Facebook and YouTube. She jumped, apparently not hearing me coming into the room. Her face was pale and sweaty, mascara had somehow made its way onto her nose.

"What's going on?" I asked, abandoning my cup and coming to sit next to her.

"I'm not sure. The party did not end the way I wanted it to."

Her cheeks were tearstained, and her lipstick was smudged. Fear shot through me and I gripped her shoulder, expecting the worse. She seemed to look herself over and laugh a little.

"Terry, nothing happened to me. It's purely emotional, I promise."

I relaxed my grip slightly and leaned back to give her some space. "Then tell me what did happen. You're scaring the crap out of me."

Macy slumped into my arms. "I was so proud. You know how I was telling you that I wanted to set up my friends? Simon and Shayla seemed to really hit it off and left the party to spend some time together. I kept imagining them looking back on that night as the beginning of their relationship. I was excited, I just let myself get lost in the party. In Britney. We were kissing, and some stupid boys started filming us."

She sat back, crying again.

"Okay, but Britney's your girlfriend? Is it a big deal you were kissing?"

Macy sighed dramatically. "Yes! You don't get it. It was like we were supposed to be on some trashy video and it made me sick. I wanted to leave, and Britney and I got into this huge fight. She told me it was time to just come out and said our friends didn't have to accept it. But it's not just our friends. It's being pigeonholed into this lifestyle like it changes who I am supposed to be. I don't want to be Macy, their lesbian friend. I am not even sure that's what I am!"

I shook my head. "You're not sure you're gay? But you love Britney?"

I saw that I was frustrating her, but I just wanted to understand. She seemed so strong and sure of herself when coming out to us two years ago.

"No, that's not what I mean. I mean that I don't feel gay. It's more than that to me, I just feel like Macy and don't like the idea of having to say that I am one thing to be happy. I am more than just that one thing."

"What does Britney think?"

Her shoulders shook with her sobs. "I am her third girlfriend. She has this all figured out and never had this doubt. She doesn't get it. She thinks that the doubt is about her, not about me. This is my first time falling in love with a girl. I don't want to have to prove it all the time. I just want to be me."

I squeezed her shoulders reassuringly. "But Mac, if you don't commit fully to this than how are you going to be able to commit fully to Britney? That's not fair to her."

Macy pushed me back, disgusted. "You don't know anything about us. What do you know? You and CJ were inseparable before the accident, and now you won't even look at him. You are hiding from him."

"That's not..."

She interrupted me. "Claire is just as bad. She's hiding from Holden and part of it is your fault. I know you always pictured having a baby first, but you aren't doing a good job of helping her feel welcome. We are all hiding."

She stormed out of the room, leaving me blushing and feeling like she had looked right through me. We were hiding, maybe it ran in the family.

*

The only time I felt like getting out of bed these days was when I was someone else. Sometimes I became her in dreams, sometimes she stole me away in the middle of the making dinner. Everything about her was in Technicolor.

She was more beautiful than me, she was loved. She didn't have past regrets hanging around her. She wasn't attempting to survive in a world without her best friend, her mom.

Despite how soft and inviting my comforter was, my phone rang with annoying beeps. I pondered how easy it would be to just toss it out the window and take a nap. But the screen read Lucy, from the office. She knew not to call unless it was important. Taking a deep breath, I accepted the call.

"Lucy? Hi."

"Hi, Terry. How are you?" she gushed, apparently happy to hear my voice.

"I'm…. Did you need something?" I asked, looking down at my dirty pajamas and feeling my greasy hair.

I was horrified even though she couldn't see me.

"Right. Well, I know you are on leave but one of your patients called. Miranda Simpson is in the hospital, and you are her emergency contact. The call was referred here, but protocol is to call you first to see what you want to do. Do you need a refresher on the patient file? I can bring it over."

I shook my head then realized that made no sense. "No, I remember her."

Miranda was barely 19. She was dating Rick, her high school sweetheart. Shortly after their junior year, he had begun abusing her. Physically and sexually. She cut herself to deal with it before we met.

I had finally convinced her to leave him and move back in with her parents. Rick scared me. He was one of those guys who was just asking for a reason to go too far.

Rick felt so much like Lucas, the abusive boyfriend of my past patient Gina. But Lucas wasn't the lone monster. Once free of Lucas, Gina murdered her mother. I hadn't seen it coming and, in some way, had assisted her by not getting her help. What if Miranda wasn't as innocent as she seemed? I didn't want to be responsible for another attack on an innocent bystander.

My throat closed, and the room spun around me. "No. Lucy, have someone else help. Take all of them."

I heard her protesting but hung up before she was able to say anything else. I sunk to where I was, shaking and crying. I tried to stand but didn't have enough strength to make it to the bed. I leaned over and pulled off the comforter, hiding underneath. I wanted to hide from it all.

I just wanted it to... stop.

*

I shook the skillet, coating the minced garlic in olive oil and smiled at Missy who sat at the dining room table.

"Being in here, watching you cook, it's hard. I still miss Marlo so much. I don't think I will ever not miss her or think about her every single day."

I nodded. "I wonder what leftovers were here when Macy and Claire came back. I can't remember what the last dinner my mom made was. But if I had leftovers, then I could have appreciated that it was the last thing that she cooked that I had the chance to eat. It should have been savored... I don't know. Does that sound stupid? It feels important."

Missy gave me a sad shrug. "Then it's important. You got the least closure after the accident. There's bound to be some feelings about that."

I shrugged but had a hard time looking her in the eye. The truth was, sometimes I hated Macy and Claire for getting to be here while her scent was still in her bedroom. I hated them for touching her things and changing anything. I hated them for being able to say goodbye. But then again, I loved them, and I needed them. I understood that part of facing my grief meant coming to terms with my sisters. I knew that, but I didn't know how to get there yet.

"Miss, I wanted to ask you kind of a weird question."

"Shoot."

I added the onions to the pan and watched them slowly turn translucent.

"What do you know about reincarnation?"

She leaned back in the chair. "Why? Do you think your mom's soul is going to come back to you?"

"No. I just... I feel weird since waking up. I was just curious."

"I don't know much, mostly just from books and conversations with others who live this kind of lifestyle. Reincarnation is supported by many religions. Sometimes it's to correct past mistakes, others believe it's just the way the world works."

"What about, what if you loved someone? Are you reincarnated together?"

"Maybe. I did read once that if someone was important to your destiny that it might change your soul. Not just lovers, but family members and such. I like the idea that if someone is your true love that you might be connected by more than just reality."

I stirred shrimp into the pot then tossed it with linguine. As Missy and I ate lunch, she shared memories, but I was lost in my intertwined memories between this existence and the past. True love was able to span more than life, I knew the weight of that truth. Maybe that's why I was so conflicted about CJ.

This life and the new part of my soul wanted him. I didn't want to deny how I felt around him. He was my first kiss and loving him forever would be easy. It was as natural as breathing. I knew that it would be effortless to fall into his arms and knew that I could trust him to take care of me no matter what.

But maybe he wasn't the "one." My past self-loved Kerry and our powerful connection had lived beyond their lifetime. Pure love made that possible. I always knew that CJ belonged to part of me, but I was a mixture of the universe. The vintage pieces of me wanted someone else and wanted to do anything to make it possible. A huge part of me loved Kerry and saw a future in his future self.

I wasn't sure what I was going to do or how CJ fit into the rest of my life. But I did know that I had to figure out who I was back then. I had to figure out how to piece my two halves together.

*

"Pizza or white cheddar?" CJ asked, holding up two different popcorn seasonings.

I shrugged and passed him the bowl of popcorn. We used to have movie nights all the time, but now alone time seemed laced with so much left unsaid. We had never talked about the days after the coma. I didn't need to be told of how he had lured me back to my body with music, I still felt the kisses he left on my forehead. Him never giving up on me meant more than I was able to put into words.

But how much did I owe him now? He believed that loving me was part of what brought me back. How did these new memories fit into that? What if Kerry's soul recognizing my own is what reconnected me with this life?

As I sat on the couch, CJ slid in the DVD and curled up next to me. Eventually, his hand found its way over to mine. I stifled a sigh as he laced his fingers through mine. When we settled in together, a vision began to filter through my mind, taking me from our downstairs living room to another kitchen years behind me.

"Kerry, this is too much," I said softly, caressing the teardrop pearl hanging from the thin white gold chain that laid in a velvet box in front of me.

"It's not. Today marks three years since we first met, and we first kissed. And we first... well," Kerry chuckled, and I laughed at his pink ears.

"Three years..." I looked up at him, searching his expression. "Sometimes it feels like nothing has changed and we are stuck in the same spot."

He wanted this to feel special, but it also opened up so much hurt in my chest. Three years and we were still meeting for hours at a time, he was still avoiding my calls and throwing away the messages his secretary left for him. I was still alone.

Kerry sat across from me. "But they aren't the same. My feelings have changed. Back then I was just blown away by how beautiful you were. Now, I am blown away by how much you get me. You're my best friend. I want to spend the rest of my life with you."

I held my breath, afraid to fracture this moment like fragile glass. He had said forever, but did it mean the same thing to both of us? I wanted the whole package. The house, the wedding, the baby and a lifetime with someone I had built my entire life around. But for the past few years, I was just a small piece of his.

"I want to be with you…" I begin, not wanting to cry.

He held me close and trailed kisses up my collarbone, each kiss making me feel precious and cared for in a way that only he was capable of.

"Then be with me. I am talking to Rachel tonight. This is ending, this week. This time next month we will be looking back on this day as our true beginning. Please say yes."

He had never offered this before. He had never chosen me back. I started crying despite the encompassing happiness I held inside of me as he fastened the necklace around my throat. He took me into his arms, kissing my collarbone and shaking a little.

"Yes. Yes, yes, yes."

"Yes?" CJ asked.

"What?" I asked, disoriented. Still being kissed by Kerry in one part of my brain. He had chosen me. I never wanted to leave that self again.

"You said yes. What's going on?"

"Nothing," I said, taking my hand back and trapping them under my leg.

"Ter, I know you well enough to recognize a vision. Where did you go? Did you see something from me?"

I knew I couldn't avoid this anymore. My stomach rolled, but I turned towards him and took a deep breath.

"CJ, I have to talk to you about something."

He sighed and looked relieved. "Finally. You have been super weird lately, but I didn't want to push you. Did I do something?"

I shook my head. "No, it's not you. It's just… when I was in a coma, I went somewhere. It changed me. When I came back, I had all of these new memories mixed up with my own. New isn't the right word, they are from a past life."

He nodded, intrigued. "That's kind of cool."

When I didn't respond, he shifted uncomfortably and crossed his legs.

"But, what does that have to do with me? You have been avoiding me."

I looked down. "It's not just memories of that life. She was in love. I have all of these memories and days with him, and it's hard to combine it with my life now."

CJ's eyebrows knit together. "What does that mean? You are in love with some guy that's dead?"

"He's sort of here too. I have feelings for him, I feel him like we were still together. I tracked him down on Facebook. I need to know where this goes."

CJ's face seemed to drain of all color, hurting him this way brought tears to my eyes. I loved Kerry, but I also loved CJ. He was my best friend and such a huge part of who I was. But I didn't want to pretend like this was less serious than it was or play down how this might affect the rest of my life and my relationship with him. He deserved more than that.

"What about us? Are we just going to pretend like this isn't crazy? I am right here Terry. I have always been right here. And you are choosing to live in this fantasy world to chase someone else?"

"You don't understand. This isn't a fantasy. Its real, it's a part of me. I don't have a choice!"

CJ stood up. "No, you don't understand. You made a choice. It's just the wrong one."

As he left the room, I looked down at the barely touched popcorn bowl. Why wasn't this easier? Love was supposed to make my world better, to create a life. Nothing about this was right or okay. I threw the popcorn across the room, satisfied with the shattering glass and mess. I laid my head back and settled within myself, wanting to go back to when I was whole.

Chapter 5

Claire

October 2015

There were a million ways I had pictured telling my future partner that I was pregnant. With a cute shirt that read Daddy, or maybe taking the test together and holding each other as it read positive.

I have always wanted kids, but I pictured being the last of my sisters to have them. I imagined being in my 30s, probably married, with a house and career under my belt. I wanted it all, and I wasn't sure if now was the right time.

I never pictured needing to tell my partner that I was pregnant in the middle of Denny's.

"That's really what you want? It's my treat," Holden said, raising an eyebrow at my single pancake without butter and syrup.

I tried to look like I was enjoying myself, but everything about this place was difficult to handle. The mixing of smells, the antiseptic from the bathroom, the bangs emitting from the kitchen. The only two things I wanted to eat these days was cold cereal and toast. Pancakes were all I was able to stomach.

I am sure that was the first sign that something was wrong. I adored breakfast food and usually put Holden to shame by eating my weight in bacon.

"You were so quiet at the movie. What's up?" he asked.

I shrugged. "I don't think you're really supposed to talk at the movies."

"That's never stopped you before."

That finally got me, and I laughed a little.

"I know, I'm sorry. It's just… I need to talk to you."

"Okay. Are you alright?"

I looked around, not wanting this noisy diner to be part of our new beginning. If this was even a beginning. My body was made of static electricity and I jumped at every bang.

"Can we take a walk?" I asked.

Holden paid the bill, and we headed out into the cold and still night. Before he could reach for me, I wrapped myself in my sweatshirt and crossed my arms.

"Claire, what's going on?"

He pulled my arm until I stopped, and we sat on a bench outside of the restaurant. The sidewalks were empty, but it still didn't feel like enough privacy.

"I just have no idea how to say this. I don't want you to hate me," I started, trying not to tear up and ultimately failing.

Holden's face went ashen, and his mouth tightened. "Are you seeing someone else?"

A laugh bubbled out of my chest, and he looked even more horrified.

"No, I'm sorry. It's nothing like that."

"Then what?"

94

I looked down at my swollen ankles and belly. I couldn't see beyond the changes and was sure Holden wouldn't be able to either.

"I'm pregnant."

Holden sat back, color coming back to his cheeks again. Now he laughed a little.

"Oh, thank God."

"Thank God?!"

He leaned forward and held my shoulders. "I thought I lost you. I have had a thing for you since high school. You were always the one. The thought of someone else… That's the worst-case scenario in my opinion."

Being in his arms and heart, this was the safest I had ever been. But part of me felt like he had lost me. Belonging to someone else this entirely was huge. It was bigger than me. So much inside of me was screaming to run and just start over. Yet, Holden was here. He was excited and looking at my belly like it was his biggest dream in the world to be a father. He looked like hope.

"I have no idea what I'm going to do," I whispered, crying.

Holden pulled me into his arms. "We will figure it out together. This isn't a bad thing. I promise. We will be okay."

I nodded and it would have been easy to be comforted by how it felt to kiss him. I knew that he was meant to be part of my life and that he loved me, he always had. But I still wasn't sure about this being right for us. How happy he was before even thinking about it scared me. How was he so sure? What was wrong with me?

As I pushed open the front door, I saw Barbara seated on the couch. She was getting more and more comfortable just being here, showing up when I least expected it.

"Bad night?" she asked.

I sighed and sat down next to her. "I guess that depends on who you ask. Holden had a great night. I... I'm not sure."

Barbara patted my leg. "It's a big decision. It has to be yours alone."

I sat back and let my head fall on the couch. "It doesn't feel like that. This life, this is part of Holden too."

"I didn't mean Holden. I meant the shadow figures."

Goosebumps broke out of my entire body. "What do they have to do with this?"

Barbara leaned back with me, taking a deep breath. "Are they still attacking you when you meditate?"

My last vision filled my mind and I had to fight off nausea. Whenever I closed my eyes and let go of this consciousness to make psychic walls, they ended up crawling all over me and tore at my skin. Their screams echoed inside of my head and their fingers groping inside of my stomach.

"They want your baby, Claire. New souls are just so... delicious."

"What can I do?" I asked, feeling protective and disgusted at her word choice.

"There's always abortion."

I sat up, shocked.

Barbara raked her fingers through her hair and shrugged. "You want to keep the baby safe. But what if you can't? Would you rather they took it instead?"

"I would rather no one took it anywhere. And that isn't my choice to make alone. This is Holden's child, he has a say in whether or not they have a right to exist," I said fiercely.

"Are you sure you mean that?" she asked, her voice biting.

"Yes!" I said, trying to keep my voice down.

"There is another way. New souls can be protected by another soul combining with them."

I sank to the couch, arching my back to relieve a knot that was forming.

"Combining with another soul? What does that mean?"

"Allowing another soul to enter you to protect this fragile, young one."

"I don't understand… like letting you possess me?"

Barbara's features clouded with what looked like concern… or anger. Her eyebrows furrowed with worry but her arms with clasped to her sides.

"I'm not a demon, Claire. I can't 'possess' anyone. It will just be a way to protect your child in a way that no one else will be able to."

I looked into her face, searching it for some kind of ulterior motive. That sounded like much more than protecting. I was still getting used to sharing my body with this baby. How safe was it to allow a supernatural spirit to enter my body at the same time?

But my mom sent her. She told me that spirit guides were supposed to know what was best for you. That what's spirit guides did.

"I'll have to think about it."

Barbara nodded firmly, looking satisfied.

*

I thought that telling Holden about the baby would be the hardest part of this whole situation, but my conversation with Barbara the night before had left me paranoid and sick to my stomach. The idea of spirits viscerally wanting my baby terrified me. I wondered how serious Holden truly was about this being what he wanted. I wondered if he worried about the future and was just playing chicken with me to see who flinched first.

"I think you should come to dinner this week. We can tell my parents together. I don't think they will be throwing us a party anytime soon, but they love you," Holden said, stopping in front of Baby Gap and casually flipping through pajamas.

"They have met me a total of four times. How do they love me already?" I asked.

I was grumpy with a migraine setting in from the fluorescent mall lights.

"Is that so hard to believe? That you are easy to love?"

I shrugged. "Maybe. It's not an ideal situation."

"It's never the right time for a baby. I was born when my parents were in their 40's."

Holden smiled and pulled out some purple footie pajamas with kites running up one side. He tried handing them to me before seeing my panicked expression. Holden carefully tucked them under one arm so that he could wrap the other around me.

"What's wrong? You think it's too early? Bad luck?"

I cringed away, shaking him loose.

"I just don't understand why you are so sure that things are going to be okay. What if it isn't? What if this is the wrong choice?!"

Holden tried to grab me again. "Because I am sure of you. I always have been."

I knew that he cared and would do anything for me. But it felt like the worst time to hear him say it out loud. I felt smothered, and panic climbed up my throat. If he was sure, then I had less permission to be afraid. If I had doubts, I was already a terrible mother.

"I'm not so positive."

He took a step back, flushing and a deep shade of crimson.

"Are you saying you don't want to keep the baby?"

"No, I am saying… I am not sure if I want to do this with… anyone else."

Holden rubbed his thighs, looking nervous. "Claire... Why? What brought this on?"

"Nothing. I just feel like I have to explore all my options. Maybe we should just… be friends for now. Until I figure out how I want the rest of my life to unfold. This is more important than just me and you."

I had been staring at my shoes, but when Holden didn't respond, I looked up. He was flushed and looked self-conscious. I had never seen him this unsure of himself. He shifted from foot to foot, and for the first time since Holden and I reconnected, I didn't feel immediately in tune with his feelings. The last thing I wanted to do was hurt him, but I also was entirely sure I didn't want anyone else telling me what to do or how I felt.

"Explore away," he said finally, turning and stalking off.

I sank down to a mall bench, exhausted and nauseous with regret. I shook my head, trying to keep my confused tears from seeping into the neckline of my shirt. I just wanted to keep my baby safe and wasn't sure who I should be afraid of.

Falling in love was the most terrifying thing that had ever happened to me. Why shouldn't I be afraid of trusting Holden? If I was alone, then there was no chance of disappointment.

Tonight, more than anything, I wished things were how they used to be. No matter how difficult things were for my family and me, Halloween was kind of sacred. It was Terry's favorite holiday, and she dressed up every year. The costume was always completely different and very creative. My favorite costume was a 70s rocker that she made in school.

If this year had been different, if I had just moved home and came to stay with them, this might have been the best year of our lives.

I needed some stability, some semblance of normalcy when I was spiraling into complete madness. Sighing, I headed into the kitchen to look for a snack. A yellowed piece of paper drew me to the small kitchen table where my mom had paid bills.

Her recipe for popcorn balls sat next to our mail. I looked for this recipe for hours when I first went through her cookbooks. It was nowhere to be found, and I wondered where she had hidden it. But I didn't have to wonder why she left it for me here now. Seeing how difficult things were between us seemed to make her terribly sad. Seeing that look in her eyes sometimes made me wish she had moved on.

I took a thankful breath, realizing that this was my peace offering, my bridge back to the Halloweens of our past and the beginning of the future. She had saved this recipe for me.

I pulled out a saucepan and began popping the popcorn while making a marshmallow, vanilla, and butter mixture in another pot. When they were done, I molded the balls carefully, setting them out on wax paper and taking deep breaths. The scent of caramelized marshmallow filled my lungs and invoked a million memories from before my parents divorced.

I placed four popcorn balls on a plate and carried them out to where Terry was sitting on the couch, staring off into space.

Nervousness tugged at my stomach. I was unsure of how she would receive this gift.

"Hey, what do you think about watching Halloweentown? I saw that it's on Disney in a couple of minutes. And... I made, these."

I sat next to her. Terry looked at the plate and looked like she might cry. She seemed to be fighting her feelings internally then tried to shake them away. Part of her didn't want to share these memories with a sister she felt betrayed by. Yet, an even more significant part of her wanted to wrap up in this tradition like a warm blanket.

Finally, she looked up and extended the blanket to me. I let out a breath and placed the plate on the coffee table, reaching over for the remote and switching it to her favorite Halloween movie.

I knew that we were forcing ourselves a little bit, we were going to have to for the first couple holidays after such a loss.

But, maybe faking it was really making it at some point. I pulled a blanket over our laps, and we crunched while getting lost in the world of magic. After a couple of minutes, the door banged open. Macy came through, her cheeks red from the fall air.

"Yes! I knew it."

Terry gave her a weird look. "You knew what? Halloweentown is on every year."

She waved dismissively in Terry's direction. Macy squeezed in between us and covered up, her fishnet tights scratching my knee.

"No, we were at Michelle's, and I suddenly craved popcorn balls. I could practically smell them. I needed to be home."

I grinned back at her. "Mom left the recipe on the table. I think she wanted us to be together."

Terry forced a grin, but suddenly another look stole across her face.

Goosebumps broke out over my arms, and warmth flooded through my chest. I held my breath. My mom always affected me this way. There was no ice in her arrival.

I saw her over Terry's shoulder. Her face was bright as she gazed down at us wrapped up together. She leaned down and put a hand on my stomach, looking excited and comforting.

I closed my eyes, wanting to share this with my sisters. I projected my gift, gently filling their minds with the vision in front of me. Terry gasped and I knew it worked. I opened my eyes slowly, focusing on keeping the connection. My mom looked at Terry and stroked her hair, she seemed concerned.

We stayed that way for a while. Macy's hand found my mothers and covered it, over my growing belly. Terry smiled and placed her hand on top of Macy's. I looked at them, fingers interlocking. It convinced me for the first time that this was right, this baby was mine. We should raise it together.

And then she was gone. But I had made my mind up. I already loved this baby, I had loved it from the moment I saw that positive test, and I needed to fight to the ends of the world to keep my baby safe.

*

The onesie I had found was not as cute as the purple pajamas Holden had picked out, but it had belonged to me. By the time I reached his house, the outfit was wrinkled from being twisted in my sweaty grip.

Finally, I took a deep breath and headed to Holden's front door to knock. When he answered, I was thankful that I didn't have to go through one of his parents and see their looks of judgment. I wondered if he had even told them because he just looked relieved to see me, despite how childish I had been.

"What's up? I thought you were a late trick or treater and was ready to give you a lecture," he said, sitting across from me on the couch.

"I probably deserve a lecture too," I said, not wanting to look him in the eye but forcing myself regardless.

He gave me a gentle grin. "Probably."

I relaxed. "I am really sorry about how I acted. I was just scared, and I took it out on you instead of talking to you about it. You being so excited made me feel like a terrible parent for being scared. It made me feel like I was unfair to the baby."

Holden shook his head. "It's normal to be scared. But you really have to stop breaking up with me whenever you get grumpy. It's really starting to bum me out."

I laughed and looked down at the onesie. "Holden, I haven't changed my mind. I am scared, and I feel more in control when the pressure is taken off of us a little bit. Having a baby ruined my parent's marriage. I don't want to lose what we have, but I have to take my time. But I am in, I want this baby. I want to raise it with you. I am in if you're in."

I gave him the onesie. He unrolled it and fingered my monogrammed name, a smile flickering across his mouth.

"I know it's mine, but my mom saved this for us, and the mall was closed. I want you to have this because it's a piece of me and I am ready to share it. I love this baby, our baby. I am scared, but I'm here," I said, my words tumbling over each other.

Holden put the onesie on the table and gently grabbed the back of my neck, pulling me close.

"I know you are. You have always been here, ready to do this. I think your heart just takes its sweet time catching up with your head. We can be… friends. But not seeing other people friends. I will give you time, but it's not easy."

I nodded. "Thank you."

"Can I kiss you? We are having a baby; this feels like a moment we should be kissing."

I grinned with my mouth against his lips, holding his lower back and letting myself melt into him. And then we were kissing, and life was perfect once again.

*

In my dream shadows stole across the floor, turning solid and making foot like impressions on the carpet next to me. I wanted to wake up, I wanted to scream, but my body was frozen like it had been so many times before. I turned, ripping myself from troubled sleep. I sighed and turned again.

Twisting in my corner pulled my attention to my bookshelf. It looked like two wisps of night fighting, turning in on each other and then tearing apart. I stifled a scream as I saw a slice of Len's face.

Shadow figures were ripping at him, trying to place their mouths over his mouth. Bodies made of smoke seemed to hold him down, and his mouth was frozen in a yell of terror. As I watched, a golden piece of light slipped from Lens mouth and into the gaping nothingness that was the shadow figures. I saw the light tremble and then just disappear.

106

I bolted to my feet, throwing my hands out and subconsciously sending out energy that shoved them away. I ran to him and gripped him by the arms, shuddering as the shadows slipped over my arms like freezing water. They dissipated, and Len fell to his knees, choking and wiping his mouth with frantic swipes.

"What the hell was happening?" I whispered fiercely.

He was shaking and jabbed a finger in my direction like he was holding a weapon.

"You ask like you have no control over preventing this from happening to me. They were stealing my light. That's how they make more shadows. They want what they don't have, light. Life."

I thought back to what Barbara told me about my baby's soul and painful goosebumps broke out on my body. I imagined Lens soul nestled in his body for the past 8 years. Him alone and fighting off the monsters that wanted to steal the sole piece of humanity that he had left.

I sat next to him, drawing him into my arms. "I am sorry Len. What should I do? I don't know how to help you."

A part of me wanted him to move on, to go into whatever light and comfort that Rusty had found. I owed it to him because he was a link back to my past and so many good memories before my parents divorced. Len was my first love, the first person to tell me that I was beautiful. At a time I felt utterly unwanted, he had been someone who made me feel like I belonged in my own skin.

As if he was reading my thoughts, Len leaned back and gently pressed his lips to mine. I pushed him away, and he seemed angry. He grabbed the back of my head, startling me with how stable he was and forcing his lips to mine. I tried to push him away, and terror began to creep its way up my spine.

I flinched as memories were pushed into my mind. How my heart raced the first time he laced his fingers with mine, braiding my hair and telling me stories from his childhood, him telling me that was the best part of his day. Then, to a darker place, my mind wasn't aware of letting me go.

When the days turned orange, and the sun left us alone at the lake. The fear I felt as Len's hand slid up my leg, going somewhere I wasn't sure I was ready to go. I tore myself from that part of my mind before I absorbed anymore of the images.

I pushed back, shaking my head slightly. "Len..."

"Please," he begged, holding me close like he had so many times those summers.

"Stop. This isn't okay," I said, forcing each word out and fighting the fear in my throat.

He glared at me before stalking out, disappearing as he crossed the threshold of my door.

Terry

October 2015

Eli had accepted my friend request almost a week ago, but I hadn't had the nerve to reach out yet. What was I supposed to say? Pretend I knew him from somewhere?

I lived in Washington, and he was from California. I had no way in to start a conversation, not even one shared hobby. But I couldn't stop looking at his photos, reading his posts with obsessive swipes. I hadn't posted anything myself in months. Being at home and recovering from a coma wasn't exactly the sexiest or most exciting lifestyle.

But the longer I waited, the more anxious I became. Something outside of me kept bringing me back to my laptop, to his profile, to memorize his new body and wonder about the old soul inside of him. Did he dream of what we had together? Did he miss something he never realized he had lost?

Before all of this happened, I had two best friends that I was able to talk to about anything. My mom was the person that I went to with my worst issues. Even if I was entirely in the wrong, she always helped me reach a solution and feel better about whatever had happened. And CJ was the person who listened to me talk until the answer just seemed to free itself from the tangle of my mind. But now... I was completely alone.

I will never be able to talk to my mom again and asking CJ about this would be incredibly cruel. Sometimes I was able to take a walk and being away from the house helped to clear my mind. Yet, I couldn't run away forever. As soon as I was alone in my room again, two souls fought inside of one still very broken body. It wasn't something I was able to turn off or walk away from.

I began typing a message. I introduced myself and told him about my accident. I tried putting into words the life that I had woken up with and how it drew me to his profile. I began asking him if he ever had déjà vu or wondered where these feelings came from. It sounded crazy. A couple of months ago, a message like this would have led to me blocking whoever sent it immediately. But he had to understand, he had to be searching the same way that I was. I took a deep breath, my fingers shaking, and pressed send.

I wanted to meditate, to contact my mom and maybe even send out my old soul in a way that called his to mine. To radiate a yearning from deep inside of me. But part of me felt like trying too hard would break this connection to whoever this other girl was.

I didn't want to risk that. If I investigated it too much, I would be left empty. It was my sole reason for breathing these days. I could look forward to this instead of trying to put the pieces of my old life back together.

*

My phone sat buzzing on the counter, but I pretended not to see it as I chopped vegetables for dinner and listened to Macy drowning on about drill team. I knew it was CJ and every time I saw his name pop up on the screen, I felt suffocated. I cared about him but wasn't ready to think about us right now.

Dealing with him was too confusing. He just made me feel terrible about wanting to pursue this thing with Eli and us fighting about it would get my sisters involved. If he didn't understand, how could I possibly explain this to Macy and Claire? Things were weird enough around them without them staring at me like I was crazy.

Macy peeked at the screen when she noticed I had zoned out.

"Are you guys fighting?" she asked.

I shrugged. "No, Mac. I am just taking some time to figure things out. To focus on me."

She raised an eyebrow at me. "Really? Because it seems like all you have been doing is avoiding your life. You won't see Lucy or take calls from the center. You won't talk to CJ. I walk into rooms and see you staring off into space. Sometimes you are even frozen in the middle of doing something. What's going on?"

I stared at her, anger surging through me and bringing a flush to my face. How dare Macy judge me? After Mom died, they encouraged Gina to kill Lucas. All of them put me in the middle of a court battle to put a former patient of mine away. If I wanted to lose myself a little bit in this other life, she of all people needed to support me. But she didn't understand at all.

When I didn't respond, Macy went on lecturing, telling me that it was time I snapped out of my mood. She said I needed to see my friends again, get back to work, get my life back together. But I didn't want any of it.

I stepped forward, taking the chef's knife from the cutting board. I plunged it into her chest. Finally, her ceaseless gabbing stopped. Her eyebrows shot up in pain. Macy flailed at me, grabbing onto the knife handle. I ripped it out and shoved it into her again. Her hands inadvertently went along with me this time.

When she dropped to the ground, I turned around and began chopping vegetables again.

"Are you even listening to me?" Macy asked.

I dropped the knife, gasping.

As I turned, I saw her standing in front of me with an annoyed expression. I looked at the ground, where she had been laying only seconds before. I panted, examining the floor for blood.

I loved my sister. Where was this anger coming from? Was I capable of really hurting her? Shaking, I wrapped my arms around my sister and hugged her tightly. I took deep breaths with vicious exhales, needing to expel the fury that had decided to take control of my body.

"I'm sorry, I'm sorry. If it's too soon, it's too soon," Macy said, startled.

She rubbed my back, wanting to comfort me. Her trying to make me feel better after what I almost did to her made me nauseous.

"No, I'm sorry Mac. I know I have been different."

Macy gave me a lopsided smile. "It makes sense, Ter. You have been through the impossible. It's kind of a miracle. I just miss you. Sometimes it feels like it's not you here with us."

If she only knew.

*

"American Baby?" I asked, tilting my head to read the magazine that Claire was reading on the screened porch.

I sat across from her and picked up the graphic novel I had meant to start.

"Yeah," she blushed a little bit. "There's so much to do, to decide. Even this early on. I can't help feeling like I am already behind."

"You're not. You are a few weeks along at most. We'll get it figured out."

She nodded reluctantly and then went back to her article. Claire might be scared, but she already glowed with the new light. Her cheeks were full of color, and her hair seemed thicker and more lustrous.

This might not be in her plan, but I wasn't in Moms. The day I reicieved my gift, she gave me a vision of the love she felt for me while I grew within her. I can't help but be a little bit envious of the connection Claire will have.

My gift lets me see a lot, but I wasn't able to see what was really happening. I wished that I was able to see what Macy did. The aura light show that had been described as layered and beautiful. I wanted to be a part of what was happening.

I wished that I knew what she was thinking in these moments when she imagined her future. It's something I hoped that I could share with her, that I wished Mom was able to share with her. Where was she planning on raising the baby? Would she move in with Holden? Was Holden even a permanent part of her future plans?

The more she settled into this pregnancy, the more secretive she became. She was going through something, maybe something to do with her gift. But she wasn't sharing anything. Perhaps she was afraid to.

I hoped that at some point that she would allow Holden in. He loved her more than anything, and she was lucky to have a partner like him. My heart broke for the both of them, seeing her having something like this in front of her but being terrified to jump in with both feet.

Holden was the man that my mom had dreamed of for us girls. He gave Claire more slack than she deserved and maybe more than she really needed. He was sweet and immediately made Macy, and I feel like family. Watching how he loved her; I was jealous in the best way. This was everything my mom had wanted for her own life and wanted for us; how could she not see that?

*

"What did you decide on?" Ash asked me, shaking a white base coat nail polish.

I pointed to a photo on her phone of a crescent moon painted over a shiny white base with silver sparkles mixed in.

She shook the bottle happily. "Good choice."

Claire had suggested instituting a spa Sunday. After finding out that it was something she and Ash had done in college, a part of me didn't want anything to do with it. I loved Ash, we had known each other for years.

But part of me thought she was the sister to Claire that I always wanted to be. I didn't want to just be an add-on to their already created traditions, I wanted to be able to make them on our own.

Regardless, I tried to enjoy my manicure. Ash was addicted to YouTube tutorials and was getting good. While she shaped and painted my nails, I turned my attention to the reality show that Macy had put on. Two women were screaming at each other. The one with badly bleached hair had seduced the brunette's husband, and now they were divorcing.

Macy shook her head. "How could you trust a man after he cheated on his wife? Even if it was with you, isn't that him proving that they can't commit to one person?"

I blushed, thinking of Kerry and the quiet secret life we had led together.

"I don't know, maybe there's more to the story. What if he was unhappy and found love in an unexpected place?" I said, casually.

Claire gave me a weird look. "Then the right thing to do is to tell your partner. There is no excuse for cheating. It's the coward's choice. I refuse to fall for someone who saw a relationship with me as an escape from his everyday life. If he leaves the first relationship, which is unlikely, there would always be the fear that he would do the same thing to you. That kind of love doesn't last."

I nodded, feeling wooden. How could she know that? A huge part of me agreed, and it felt like a familiar argument. This was something I had asked myself a million times in my previous life. But there was no denying the fact that it felt like Kerry was made for me. As ashamed as I was, they weren't able to understand falling in love this way.

"I read once that Johnny Depp said that if you fall in love with two people you should always choose the second because if you truly loved the first, then you couldn't have fallen in love with the second," Macy said, looking thoughtful with a mouthful of Cheetos.

I nodded. "I agree with that."

Ash and Claire shared a quick look then busied themselves with cleaning up the nail polish bottles. Was it that obvious?

If I had really loved CJ, would I have been able to fall in love with Kerry? Or were my two loves superimposing over each other? What if both of them were the one true love of the two separate people that made up my existence? How was I supposed to choose?

I thought of my mom telling me to be kind and was ashamed of myself. I didn't mean to be unkind, to Claire or to

CJ. I didn't expect to be angry with Claire when she needed support. I didn't mean to hurt CJ; he hadn't done anything but love me. But I needed to finish this journey if I was ever going to find myself again. I needed to meet Eli to see how it felt to be with him so I was able to make sense of how it felt to be with CJ. I needed to make myself happy for once.

Chapter 6

Claire

November 2015

I could imagine a life with Holden but felt like we were starting it out of order. What love story ended happily when it started with an unplanned pregnancy?

As the ultrasound wand explored my body, Terry held my hand. The last couple of months had been super strange between the two of us, and I wasn't sure how to bridge the gap between now and how it had been when we were kids. But one thing hadn't changed. Terry was still my comfort.

"If you look right over here, there is what looks like a gray circle. That's your baby's heart."

My mouth dropped open as I absorbed the beauty in front of me. Inside of me. Terry squeezed my fingers, and I saw that she was crying with her gaze fixed on the screen. I saw the curve of my child's head, the spidery line of their spine, their little toes and leg bones. I couldn't help but think that I already recognized my nose and hoped they didn't inherit my height. My heart beat along with that little heart on the screen, and I was overcome by such a rush of love. Of completeness.

"Are you able to tell when she is due?" Terry asked.

"May 25th. Congratulations, again."

She printed out a small photo and gave it to me before giving me some privacy to get dressed.

"How do you feel?" Terry asked, a huge smile making her look like herself for the first time in months.

"I don't even know. Excited. Scared. Mostly excited."

On the way home we got milkshakes, my latest craving was raspberry and caramel ice cream. I took a little doughnut magnet my mom bought in California from our kitchen drawer and stuck the ultrasound on the fridge for Macy. As I dreamily turned around, Barbara appeared in front of me so quickly that I choked on a mouthful of whipped cream.

"Barbara! Hi, you scared me."

She sneered at me, looking over my shoulder at the ultrasound.

"I thought we talked about this."

"About what?" I asked, feeling ashamed of myself for some reason.

"This whole *baby* situation. You can't go around acting like you are normal, that this is a normal pregnancy. If you don't protect yourself and take care of this problem, you will allow those shadow figures to enter our world through your body."

"No, I am not going to let that happen…" I started, setting my milkshake on the counter.

"How are you going to protect yourself?" she asked, her chest heaving.

I stared at her. Barbara's cheeks flushed, and her image shook in and out of my vision. She was more than worried. She was jealous. I wondered, not for the first time, if she wasn't able to have children. There was more to her backstory, and this pregnancy seemed like an inconvenience to her. This baby wasn't just a risk to my health, but a betrayal to her somehow. From the moment she found out about the baby she had been against it. My mom had never mentioned her pregnancies being more dangerous because of her gift, how could Barbara be so sure?

"I am going to do whatever it takes," I told her.

"Claire, stop being a child!" she screamed, ripping the photo off of the fridge and swiping all of the dishes off of the counter.

Terry rushed into the room; her fists were clenched like she was expecting an intruder. She looked around, seeing me on the opposite side of the room from the destruction.

"What's going on?" she asked.

Barbara circled her, looking like a predator.

I tried to calm her down, reaching out to her even though my hands went through her like smoke. Terry's eyes were wide as she watched me, I knew looked like a lunatic talking to myself.

"You get rid of it, or you let me in. If you don't, you will never be able to save another soul again. You won't be able to move anyone on or help them find their way. You will invite those monsters into your body and into your home. This pregnancy will destroy you. This baby is making you weak," Barbara said, spitting with each vicious statement.

I sank down against the counter, my palms sinking into the raspberry jam swirled through my previously celebratory dessert. Terry squatted beside me. Her eyes danced around me like she was searching for a wound, something to put a Band-Aid on.

Barbara was there, stamping around the room, and then she was gone. Her screams were gone, but I still felt her accusations. I felt her doubt. I was filled with even more fear than before.

I wasn't afraid of this pregnancy so much as afraid of Barbara's mood swings. I was beginning to wonder if my mom had made a mistake, or if she even sent Barbara at all. Maybe she knew something about spirits and unborn souls that my mom couldn't tell me, but that didn't feel true in my gut.

Something else tickled the back of my mind. Barbara had said that souls needed to merge with a new one to be reborn. She was distancing me from Holden because he believed in the good of this pregnancy. Barbara told me that she was the only person I had in my corner. But her sole suggestions were murdering the child I was already in love with or entering my body to protect it.

Maybe I wasn't the one who needed her. Perhaps she chose me as her way to enter the world for whatever business she had left unfinished in her lifetime. Spirit guides were supposed to fill you with strength. But all Barbara did was confuse me and make me feel like a failure in every aspect. The shadow figures were able to access me even more than before. Maybe she was bringing them to me. Perhaps she was one of them.

"Terry, I have to talk to you," I said in a thin voice.

*

"At three months your baby is about the size of a tube of Lifesavers," Ash said, turning What to Expect When You're Expecting so that I was able to see the diagram.

I touched my belly affectionately. "Terry said that the baby looked like a little mermaid on the ultrasound."

It was amazing to think of all of the changes that were quietly going on inside of my body. The process just seemed perfect and intricate; it was beautiful. It was the first time in a long time that I believed there might be an actual God out there somewhere. Being able to create an entire child was awe-inspiring and humbling.

Ash sat up and rested her back on her bedroom wall. "Speaking of ultrasounds, this Barbara stuff is getting pretty crazy. Have you decided how you are going to handle it?"

I was almost relieved to be talking about Barbara instead of the status of things with Holden. Ash was really upset that we were slowing things down. She wanted so much for us to be a happy little family. She wanted to be sure enough for the both of us.

"I don't know. She's supposed to be my spirit guide. I am supposed to trust her. She said that my mom sent her," I began, wanting to hear what she thought before I said anything else.

"She's not a person at all. How do we know that she is who your mom is talking about? She could have been trolling your house waiting for an opportunity to reveal herself."

I nodded, taking a huge bite of ice cream. "But why? She keeps saying that she is trying to save me. Why would she tell me to get rid of the baby if she was planning on taking it's place in this world? That doesn't make any sense."

Ash closed the book, her face going a waxy yellow. "But how did you feel when she approached abortion?"

"I immediately wanted to do anything to protect my child."

"Exactly. Maybe even desperate enough to allow a spirit to enter you to protect them from the shadow figures. If she was patient and was able to slowly work on your emotions, you being afraid worked in her favor."

My stomach churned as I let that sink in. If she wasn't here to help me, how did she find me at all? Besides a second chance, what did she want from me?

*

Holden had stayed over after helping us grocery shop for Thanksgiving and having him here finally cleared my head enough to write for the first time in weeks. I put in my earphones and scrolled through my outline and early chapters.

My young heroine spent her days watching her glamourous neighbor from her backyard and bedroom window. The more I read about this beautiful woman, the more I realized that I saw Barbara more often than I initially thought. She was already a ghost when I introduced myself to her, and she kept going through the motions of her daily life.

When I saw a man visiting her house, I was seeing her projections of the life she left behind that she missed the most. She was stuck here while the man that she loved moved on and created a life without her. She was stuck with no one but a precocious little girl who spied on her.

I read about the young girl. She felt misunderstood and was so desperate for an escape. She locked herself in her room to daydream about her neighbor and spent her days at the lake. I began reading chapters I didn't even remember writing for the first time, recognizing that I was calling to whoever was attempting to get through in the house. I wanted to make sense of these nightmares and set this scared childfree.

Goosebumps broke out over my body as I absorbed passages of being touched under the falling sun, wanting to tell someone but feeling a perverse sense of secrecy and specialness. The little girl feeling like she had found someone who really cared about her when she needed it most. Feeling ashamed of herself for not knowing the rules to this new and terrifying game. Suddenly Len popped into my mind, and my muscles were frozen in space.

The line of his brow and the callus of his thumbs came back to me. I felt him wrap himself around me. The face this little girl was afraid of came closer into focus.

I didn't just see this little girl anymore. I was inside of this little girl, living these memories. The room in front of me shifted like I was on an amusement park ride and the gears in my brain finally allowed me to see the entire picture. It had been Len, bringing me to the lake and pulling me far beyond what was okay. It was Len taking my shirt off and kissing my stomach, pushing his fingers inside of my shorts and underwear until I sobbed. It was Len.

My stomach rolled and clenched with nausea, making me sweat. I had called to a child, allowing them to open up to me so that I heard them more clearly. But it had been me all along. These were my dreams, my nightmares. This was my intuition warning me that Len had more power over me than I had ever given him credit for.

More than that, Barbara had known even back then and had chosen not to protect me. I remembered talking to her on these afternoons, wanting to explain what was happening, hoping she knew what to do. Wishing she could save me.

Instead of telling me to let my mom know, she watched me as I talked and enjoyed the pain I was experiencing. She fed off of it and waited for me all of these years. Not to help me, but to watch me drown. She had gone out of her way to get a front row seat to the second showing.

Who was she? I didn't leave her the way that I had left Rusty. Why would she be picked to be my guardian when she had no intention of protecting me? What happened to her when she was alive to make her so twisted and angry?

My first instinct was to tell Holden, to have him hold me like he did when I confided to him about my family's gifts. But this was different. This wasn't something I didn't have control over.

A sick guilt overcame me whenever I thought about it. A part of me felt like I gave Len permission to use me this way. I didn't want the way Holden looked at me to change. I didn't want him to feel as disgusted as I did right now. I didn't want Holden to find that this was his deal breaker.

*

"I'm not sure it's supposed to look this," Macy said, stirring the cranberry sauce with a grimace.

I shared a look with Terry, trying not to laugh. I might have wanted to carry on Mom's memory through food, but Macy didn't seem to have the skill or desire to learn. She ruined every meal that she tried to help with and I was starting to wonder if she was doing it on purpose so that she didn't have to make Thanksgiving dinner with us.

It was exhausting and long work, but when Terry was chopping vegetables and basting the turkey, she looked like herself. She didn't fade away and disappear into whatever reality she had been escaping too lately. She told stories about us from when we were younger, a smile looking easy on her lips for the first time in forever.

"You're absolutely right. That is cranberry soup. How did you crush every single berry? You have been stirring that for maybe two minutes," Terry said, peering into the saucepan before taking it from Macy.

Macy smirked. "I guess I am just no good at this. Maybe I should just go watch TV."

I sighed dramatically before waving her away. Britney and Holden were in the living room watching the Macy's Thanksgiving Day Parade. It was super strange for CJ not to be here, but Terry finally came clean and told us about the guy she had contacted through Facebook.

Macy wanted to believe that this whole thing was romantic, the way she woke up with him in her heart. But I couldn't help but feel terrible for what CJ was going through and was afraid of how dangerous this all was. I hated it but had to let Terry make her own decisions. I guess that's how they felt about the weirdness between Holden and me.

"I think we need some chicken stock. I am going to see if Safeway is open," Terry said, squeezing my shoulder before grabbing her purse.

"This is one thing I miss, being able to eat. My mom used to make the best stuffing," Len said from behind me, making me jump.

Ever since that night with the shadow figures, I had been dreaming of him. I remembered so much as soon as our lips touched that night. I remembered wanting him but not understanding what that truly meant. I saw all of those memories through the eyes of an adult and was horrified.

I remembered pushing him away when the kisses got too intense. He kept forcing his tongue into my mouth and it made my stomach clench in the worst way. He made his way into my shirt without asking if it was okay. He had slid his hands into my shorts and forced his fingers into me, thinking that my tears were of pleasure and ignoring my pain.

He hurt me over and over, telling me that he loved me and that this was how things were supposed to be. The pain seemed to be what my mom had carried with her from her relationship with my dad. I believed him.

I didn't know he knew better, because if he genuinely cared about me, he wouldn't have been able to ignore my tears to satisfy himself. I hadn't stopped coming because of my dad, I used it as an excuse to escape from a situation that nauseated me.

I had no idea how to talk to Len now. Seeing him made me sick, but I had promised to move him on. Maybe that was the one way to really be free of him. I wished it was as easy as being able to lock him out or call the police on him when he hung around the house. But no one else saw him, I was utterly alone in this.

"Why are you here?" I said casually, turning from him but also being afraid of having my back to him.

"You know what else I miss?" he asked, slinking over to me, enjoying how uncomfortable I was.

I shrugged, wanting him to leave.

As he slipped his arm around my waist and leaned into my shoulder, I froze with fear. My skin felt like it wanted to crawl right off of my body. Len breathed on my shoulder where my shirt revealed my bare collarbone.

"I miss being able to touch you... Remember? I know you do. The more, connected we were, the more I was able to actually feel you. The stronger your emotion, the stronger the experience was."

I tried to shrug him off, but I was paralyzed. "The more afraid I was, the more you could hurt me?"

He snarled at me, his teeth looking wet and inhuman "Afraid? I don't remember you ever telling me to stop. Those memories are what kept me here, waiting for when you came back to play. They were more than enough to keep me entertained in the meantime."

Len rubbed the front of his jeans, reminding me of another aspect of our days together. Bile rose like panic in my throat.

130

"What the hell?"

I spun, seeing Holden in the doorway of the kitchen. Seeing him see Len. I stared at them, watching them size each other up. Then Len was gone.

"Did you see him?" I asked, exasperated.

"Of course, I did. I heard you from the kitchen. Reaching for me. Why did you force me to see that? I know you aren't sure about us, but are you really using your abilities to cheat on me?!"

I ran to him, reaching for his wrists as he was ripping them away from me.

"Holden no, please," My words tumbled over each other.

If he was able to see him, then I wasn't alone in what Len was doing to me. Maybe it was my pregnancy, maybe I was able to project in a new way as my hormones surged through my body. Either way, I didn't have to do this on my own.

"Are you using him to escape? Do you hate the idea of having a family with me that much?" Holden asked, his voice was watery and defeated.

"Of course not. This whole thing is not what you think."

"Then explain."

And for the first time since that summer, I could. And I did.

*

Macy cried as I finished talking. I was ashamed of myself. For talking myself into ignoring these memories and placing all of the blame on my family instead. I felt embarrassed to be able to give them the horrible details of that year for the first time. I wanted them to understand why I hid it from them, it was a shame that I still weighed heavily on my heart.

Terry turned red, her freckles making her skin splotchy and uneven.

"You do understand that you made this Mom's fault, right? You were so damn sure that you were different that you would rather let yourself be molested than tell her that you had a gift?"

I looked at my chipped fingernail polish. "Terry, I never wanted this to happen. I just wanted to feel loved. I thought Len cared about me. I didn't realize what was really happening."

"But you knew enough to know that you wanted to keep it a secret. That you wanted Mom to feel responsible for pushing you away. She died believing that she ruined your life, but you did a good enough job of that all on your own," she spat.

Macy strode across the room and slapped her, leaving an imprint on one cheek.

"Fuck you, Terry. Mom is gone, but Mom can see into Claire's heart now and would have never made her feel like shit for being victimized. How dare you try to justify it?"

I covered my mouth with a fist, bawling.

Terry flushed, "You're right, I'm sorry. I'm just shocked. This is all... a lot."

132

Macy dropped to her knees and pulled Terry into her arms. "But breaking us apart isn't helping us at all. Claire needs us. You have to leave your crap at the door and come through for us."

She nodded, hugging Macy back. They agreed to help me get through this, but I still felt like an outsider looking into their home and feeling like a burden with all of this emotional baggage. After a while, I convinced them to take a walk so that Terry had a chance to calm down and Holden and I had enough privacy to talk.

"I know this might feel like the worst timing in the world, but this makes me want to move in even more than before. To protect you," he said, looking tortured and ill.

"To be here? In this house?"

"Yes, in this house. With you. I know you find yourself unlovable and feel responsible for the heartache in your family. But that's not what I see when I look at you, Claire. I don't see a victim; I don't see whatever you think your sisters see. I see *you.* I see you, and I love you. I want to move in, even if that doesn't mean into your room right now. I want to love you; I want to raise this baby with you and be here when you need me. For whatever."

It was exactly what I needed to hear right now, that my past didn't push Holden away or cause him to find me disgusting. But it didn't make it any easier to say yes. Especially now, I had a lot of feelings to work through and didn't want to jump back into a relationship to put distance between me and my pain. If I didn't deal with this now, my literal ghosts would haunt me forever. I needed to grow a little more, on my own, before I could be the wife and mom I wanted to be.

"Give me time, please."

Holden sighed, but leaned in and stamped a gentle kiss on my lips.

"You know, we have other options," he told me.

"What do you mean?" I asked.

"Again, not the best time, but there's always my house."

"With your parents?" I said, trying not to laugh.

He saw my expression and chuckled. "I guess that sounds pretty silly. But… my dad isn't feeling great, and I decided to start buying the house from them."

"Is it bad?" I asked, sitting next to him and rubbing his back.

Holden nodded; his brows drew together. "It really is. The doctors don't think there is much to do this time. I didn't want him to have to worry about a mortgage payment on top of all of his medical bills. We don't have to live there, but I am buying it. There's always that as an option."

I kissed his cheek and took a deep breath of his cologne, letting it ground me. I didn't want to leave. I had fought this transition tooth and nail, but it was my home. At the same time, raising a child in a house I shared with my sisters was just as unconventional as raising one with Holden's parents.

It scared me that he was willing to take such a big step with no reservations, that he believed in us that much. He wouldn't regret it, it wasn't him. Holden gave his all because it was who he was.

When his dad got cancer for the first time the summer after high school, he had given up his college dreams without a second thought and took over working at the grocery store. He stayed home to help his parents, and his dad beat it. But Holden wasn't interested in school anymore. He had made his life here, in his childhood home, falling in love with his customers and owning a business. It was his father's life, and he felt blessed to be able to pay back the man who had always been his best friend.

"You are so… good. You know that right?" I told him.

Holden beamed at me, his whole face lighting up with his grin. "I know. I am a catch. Lucky you."

I laughed and nudged him. He caught my arm to pull me close and gently kiss me.

"You are good too. And we are good together, better than we are apart. Let me prove it you."

I nodded but still carried fear and reservation in the pit of my stomach. He was terrific, agreeing to share my life with him wasn't a fair bargain when all I brought to the table was pain.

Terry

November 2015

"Hey, I got a flyer in the mail about the senior winter dance. Do you want to shop for a dress this weekend?" I asked Macy, turning to her after setting the spaghetti sauce to simmer.

Macy blushed and shook her head. "No. I don't have a date."

I sat across from her. "What about Britney? Are you guys still fighting?"

She ran her hand over face, smearing her make up.

"We actually had another huge fight, she called me a part-time lesbian then asked a guy named Ray to the dance. She said she wanted me to see how it felt to have her pretend like it meant nothing."

I gasped quietly. "That's terrible Mac, I am so sorry."

Macy shrugged. "It's not like anything could get any worse these days. I finally talked to Shayla about the party that started all of this. It's true. Simon forced her to go down on him. She was scared that he is going to come after her again. I tried convincing her to tell the counselor, but she isn't ready. I can't tell and make it her word against mine. But it might have happened to another girl by now, or worse, he might not have stopped there."

"Do you want me to go with you and talk to the counselor?" I offered.

I was sweaty, and my heart pounded. This was the closest I had come to my old job in months, and even the idea of it made me feel like I was going to have a panic attack.

"No, not yet. I have to get Shayla on board first."

I nodded, hating myself for feeling relieved.

"I just feel like all of this is my fault," Macy said.

She ran her palms over her already wrinkled outfit.

"How?"

"I thought their auras belonged together. I set them up."

I shook my head. "No, Mac. People have free will. Simon was already this kind of person. He has probably done this to other girls."

"How are we supposed to help people if we can't be totally sure? I mean, this happened right in front of us when we were growing up, and we had no idea."

Claire's tortured face as she told us about Len was still fresh in my mind, and I blushed. I was so embarrassed by my initial reaction. I just couldn't be around her these days, no matter what she did it was easy for me to be angry with her. I had no control over myself and this darkness just kind of took over.

"I know, I feel awful."

Macy caught my eye like she was feeling out how serious I was. It was hard to accept that a part of her wanted to protect Claire from me.

"Len is a ghost. How can we protect her from him?" Macy asked, her voice cracking.

"We will figure it out. I promise," I told her, giving her a kiss on the head and then standing up to finish dinner. I kept my back to her to hide my tears.

*

I never understood how much weight the color black held until coming home from the hospital. When I was going through physical therapy, the black was there, tempting in that it promised me safekeeping if I chose to pass out instead of pushing through the pain. It was there as I tried to live my life, darkening the edges and reminding me that I would never be able to climb out of this hole completely.

The one thing I looked forward to right now was emailing Eli. He was the only part of my life that was full of light, enough light to burn through all of this black turmoil.

Terry,

I am not this person, but I must be because I am writing this message in the first place. Do we know each other? Ever since you friend requested me, I have been coming across your profile over and over. You haven't posted in half a year, and still. I have been going through your photos, wondering why you are so familiar. I know your smile.

I'm not sure how that's possible since I grew up in California and you are in Washington. But it's true. I have been dreaming of you, having déjà vu of moments that are impossible.

Please don't think that I am crazy or some kind of stalker. I don't want to scare you. I am not trying to get anything out of you, but I also kind of feel like you understand. Maybe you have these feelings too?

-Eli

I had read the message over and over, feeling like a 16-year-old and wanting to print it out and carry his words in my pocket. I wanted to touch them with my fingertips instead of just through my computer screen. I had memorized his feelings, his feelings about me.

I knew that this was bigger than me. I wondered if he had an accident as well. Or maybe mine was enough to wake up the universe. Maybe my old soul just needed to be shaken and had sent out a siren call. A call loud enough to emit through three states, to bring us back together.

I stared at the screen for more than an hour. It took that long for me to get the courage to write back, but I knew that I had no choice. It felt like the conclusion my life had been leading to from the very beginning.

Eli,

I woke up with all of these feelings. Feelings and memories from another person, another lifetime, as crazy as that sounds. I remember Kerry and Barbara being in love and wanting to make a life with each other. The pearl necklace he gave her and how it felt to be held by him.

I woke up with your name on my lips. But not just who you are now, you as Kerry. Does that make any sense to you?

This is crazy. But it feels right. Us being able to talk about this makes me feel the sanest I have felt in a long time.

-Terry

*

We had always celebrated CJ's birthday in the same way, but it had never been forced until this year. A midnight movie at the theatre that shows black and white films on Tuesdays then fries and milkshakes from Sally's.

We began this tradition in high school when we didn't have any money and staying out until 3 am was the one allure we needed to make the night epic. But it had turned into more than that for us. CJ's birthday always ended up changing things for us one way or another.

When we were 13, we had kissed for the first time in his backyard. That year we walked to Sally's, a drive-thru hamburger stand across the street from a park. It was our favorite for so many reasons, just one being that they sold the best caramel milkshakes in town made with real toffee. We also loved it because it was a short walk from both of our houses.

We had taken our milkshakes to the swings, and the swings reminded us of our first kiss, it was a kiss that led to many that night. That led to my first French kiss. I still tasted the caramel from CJ's tongue, it was the most intimate thing I could imagine at the time.

When we were 16, it led to making out in his brand-new car. The car where we christened his back seat in a way that still made me blush. We both agreed that falling into bed with each other was a mistake. I loved CJ so much that sometimes it made it easier to make decisions that I wasn't sure I was ready for.

But there were never any regrets because he was CJ. He was my childhood, he was every happy memory from high school, and he was my first love in a way that was like pure serendipity. I didn't regret that he held every first I was capable of giving to him because he cherished each one.

We had slept together a handful of times since then, the last being when we were 18. I was living in my dorm room at school. It was his birthday, of course. I was home on Thanksgiving break, and we ended up at the park.

My sisters would be scandalized to find out that we had made love in the park, cushioned with pine needles and the dewy grass. But it was the most authentic moment of my life.

CJ was all the things I wanted in a partner and more. He was more concerned with how to make my body sing than his, bringing me to the brink fulfilled him in the most carnal way.

It was terrific but changed our relationship permanently. That night we tasted forever, and both knew that if we were to go there again, there was no coming back. CJ had patiently waited for that moment, and sometimes I let myself admit that it was where my life was headed from that very first kiss.

But I hated thinking that it was something I didn't have a choice in. Loving him was so easy that it took no faith. It was a done deal, and I hated it sometimes. I didn't always feel this way, but now all I was able to think about was that love had to

143

be a little bit of blind faith because you weren't supposed to know for sure.

I wanted adventure, I wanted to have to jump with my eyes closed and have no idea how it was going to turn out. A tiny piece of me wanted drama because lasting relationships needed that little bit of mystery. Was it possible for CJ and me to really continue when we had just been comfortable? It was destined to fizzle out if it was that easy.

Regardless, I was terrified of tonight. We had made it through the movie, but CJ seemed like he was working himself up to something. The walk to Sally's was short and extended in the worst way. Things had been stilted, and I struggled to find something to say. This was our tradition, something I looked forward to all year long. But now I couldn't see myself in this moment or in my life. This night was about change us, whether I liked it or not.

CJ carried my milkshake over to one of the picnic tables, where I insisted on sitting. Here in the lights from the drive-thru, I tried to push away the magic that always seemed to find us.

I decided to close off the part of myself that still wanted CJ in whatever form. I want didn't go to the park because tonight was supposed to be something else. Tonight, might be a beginning.

"Another year gone. I can't believe we are almost 30," CJ said, taking a huge drink and shivering like he always did.

"I know. We are going to have to celebrate that in a big way."

He shrugged. "I don't know. My birthdays usually end in a pretty great way. It usually feels pretty big."

I swallowed, my milkshake feeling a hundred times thicker in my swollen throat.

Maybe he took my silence for agreement because he leaned in for a kiss. Like he had a million times before. Like I had wanted him to a billion times before.

Except now, Eli was a connection to a life I wanted even more. It was a life where I wasn't a girl who had lost her mom and was struggling to get out of bed in the morning. I had two loves in my heart and maybe this lifetime wasn't big enough for both of them. Something had stolen Eli away from me before we got our big ending, CJ might disrupt whatever cosmic encounter I had stumbled upon.

Right before our lips met, I put my hand up to his chest to stop him. "Don't."

"Don't? Seriously?" CJ said, wanting to laugh but blushing instead.

I sat back, uncomfortable. "CJ, please. I tried to explain."

"About your ghost man? About the stranger you met online?"

How he sneered hurt my heart, but I nodded anyway.

"He's not a stranger. His name is Eli. He contacted me. He has been having the same feelings, this is going somewhere."

CJ's face changed from incredulous to a pain that almost made me change my mind. His expression hardened despite his angry tears and he clenched his cup so hard I was afraid the shake was going to shoot out of the straw.

"What about us Terry? What about me."

I looked down, still a coward. Looking him in the eye made this impossible to say.

"What about us, CJ? You were never mine, to begin with. You were never my boyfriend. You had girlfriends growing up. You don't belong to me, and I don't belong to you."

I wanted that to be true, but how my heart felt right now told me that it was a half lie at the least. CJ was so silent that I looked up. He was pale, and for a moment I thought he was going to pass out.

"Fine, Terry. Belong to yourself. But I am moving on. I can't do this half shit anymore. I wasted enough time on it already, wasted enough of my life. Please don't contact me until you figure this out. I can't be your doormat or be the second choice if this doesn't work out."

He stood up, threw his milkshake at the trashcan and stalked off, leaving me alone at the picnic table we had never sat at before. He was out of the picture. Now I could really focus on my future. This is what I wanted, so why did I feel like I was dying inside?

*

"Here we go. That was amazing, Ter. You must be exhausted" Macy said, settling me on the couch and sitting next to me so that she was able to take off my shoes.

"How did it go?" Claire asked, hanging a dishtowel over a dining room chair.

I sighed. Physical therapy had gone great. I was finally able to walk alone for the first time since June. It was a significant accomplishment on my very last day of physical therapy.

However, having to work through this kind of inescapable pain drained me emotionally. My bones seemed made of concrete, and every movement scraped my skin from the inside.

"She walked! Alone, all the way across the room," Macy said, clapping a little.

"That's great! Soon you'll be back to your old self," Claire said, squeezing my shoulder.

I shook my head, tears trailing over my cheeks, and I hung my head.

"No, this doesn't change anything," I mumbled.

It all seemed to crash down on me at once. I might be getting better, but my life would never be the same. I would never be the same.

"Ter?" Macy asked, reaching to touch my knee.

"Things won't be the same! Mom isn't here! I can't go back to work, no one trusts me," I yelled, leaning back against the couch as my back screamed in protest.

My sisters stood, frozen and shocked at my outburst.

"Maybe when the trial is over..." Claire tried.

I sat up. "No. What will change? Catherine will still be dead, despite how hard Mom worked to protect her. And Lucas is still dead and unable to go to jail for what he did. You two made sure of that."

They would have to appear in court as well, but their testimony would only strengthen Gina's story. What about justice for me?

Forcing myself to stand up, I went to the kitchen. I grabbed a bottle of wine out of the fridge on my way down to my room. I couldn't go back in time to regain what they had stolen from me, but sometimes I was able to forget for a few hours. Sometimes enough wine let me believe none of this had happened at all.

Chapter 7

"Are you ready to meditate?" Barbara asked, appearing for the first time since freaking out over the ultrasound.

Just the sight of her made me nervous and I had no idea how to react. She seemed to want to continue our relationship like nothing happened, but there was no way I trusted her anymore.

"I have a question first," I said, trying to center myself and watch her reactions.

"Okay," she responded, trying to appear nonchalant.

"Did you know what Len was doing to me?" I asked.

Her answer was so important to me, but I was still nervous to hear what she had to say. I remembered telling her what was happening and her just standing by. She never tried to protect me or encourage me to get help. Why would she be my spirit guide after betraying me like that?

She nodded carefully, "I did. You told me that an older boy was interested in you and that you were really confused about what was happening. But I didn't know that it was Len, he wasn't attached to the house until you regained your gift."

A piece of me wanted to find comfort in that, but it was too easy. Len was here now, why hadn't she warned me?

149

"Claire, you didn't realize I was a ghost back then. How could I have helped you?"

I shrugged, feeling more confused than before. I had tried contacting my mom to talk to her about the whole thing, but it was white noise. For now, it looked like I was stuck with her. I reluctantly sat across from Barbara and we began working on my brick wall.

"Claire, please focus," Barbara said, cracking open one of her eyes.

My mind defenses were still shaky and morning sickness was a hard thing to ignore. I was tired all of the time and starving despite not being able to eat anything. I nodded at her and exhaled slowly to relax my body. I tried to imagine my wall, but I was being pushed away from it.

"It's not working," I said, deflating.

"It's easy to see why. After all of this time, you still don't trust. You aren't letting me in. I can help you build this wall if you open yourself up to me, Claire."

I looked at my shoes, unsure. "I am trying."

"No, you're not!" She circled me like a wild animal, angry again.

"I am…"

She cut me off. "Do you want to save your baby or not?"

I flushed with a dull fear, and I concentrated on refocusing. I wasn't sure what Barbara wanted from me, but I did know that she had let me be hurt in the past and didn't have my best intentions in mind. I didn't think she wanted to save my baby. I think she wanted me as a conduit. I looked inward and searched within my memories and the shadowland for Barbara's true intentions, why she was sent to me.

My skin prickled as she swept over me, entering my mind. I tried to imagine the brick wall, but I was pushed even harder back than before. I started to have the feeling that the brick wall wasn't the issue, it wasn't the most important thing happening here. I turned around in my mind, feeling like I was moving through wet cement.

I was in the middle of a graveyard, standing beside a crumbling wall. This wasn't my mind. It never had been. Barbara had been leading me further and further into the shadowland. A dusty gray desert spread before me. However, there were no shadows to be seen. I heard the hissing of their cracking fingertips as they scraped over my skin. But I couldn't see them. I gasped as my stomach rolled fiercely, something rolling that was too big to be my child.

I put my hands over my face, terrified of what I might see behind the veil of my eyelids. Shadows twisted inside of me, let in by my ignorance. They squeezed my womb, treading their way inside, their jaws chomped at my child inside, missing over and over, tearing off pieces of each other instead. I screamed, grasping my stomach like I was able to open it and thrust them out.

Barbara appeared before me. "There is a way, a way to keep them out forever."

I shivered, looking at what she held. A glistening ice pick, the tip so sharp that it lit up like a siren call. Her eyes locked on mine. I watched her pupils open until they were a black hole. Dirty reaching fingers into my own eyes, taking me over.

She was looking at me, but it didn't feel like I was the person she was seeing in front of her. Tears streamed down her sore cheeks, and her body shook. I was seeing this Barbara, fierce and imposing. But I was also seeing her crying, huddled in a bathroom. Not over a negative pregnancy test, but someone else's positive test. I saw her wanting to kill another child that was standing in her way. This was always her plan. Not to possess me to protect my baby, to own me to get rid of it once and for all.

I reached forward and the ice pick brushed against my palm. Then it was in my hand, and I was lifting the edge of the nightgown I was wearing. I was tracing the pick against my inner thigh, wondering how far I needed to push it inside of me to rid me of the demons that wanted to devour me from the inside out.

"Do it, let me in, or end it now," Barbara hissed, licking her lips with anxiousness.

The ice pick caught on my panties, it would only take a single rough jerk to finish this once and for all.

I shrieked again as smoldering hands shook my shoulders. I felt like my lashes were hot glued shut and forced them open, seeing that I was in my living room once again. I screamed and focused all of my power into force, throwing Barbara away from me. She hit the wall opposite the TV, smashing the painting Macy had hung the week before.

I stared at her, my mouth hanging open and my throat raw from her nails clawing their way inside of me. She glared, her body flickered from stable to a wispy black over and over. I saw for the first time that she was made of rays and that her beams held the same darkness the shadows carried around them. She had brought them to me, she wanted them to hurt me. She tried to hurt me.

I touched my shoulders, where fingerprints had burned marks onto my skin. Len sat next to me, seething at Barbara.

"I told you! She's mine! What the hell are you doing?" he screamed.

Nausea flowed through my body, and I had to fight for consciousness. With my mind still this open, I had no idea what might happen to me if I gave into the black that touched the edges of my vision.

Barbara's chest heaved. "This is bigger than you, Len. I need her, I need what's inside of her. If there is no baby, nothing is keeping me from Kerry. It's the answer to everything."

They fought, and it took all of the strength I had to hold onto the carpet. I made it to my knees, and dry heaved. Black spots grew in my vision as I struggled to breathe through the nausea choking me. Eventually, Len patted my back.

"She's gone, you're okay," he said quietly.

I looked up at him and he flickered in the same way.

"What did you mean, I'm yours?" I asked between gasps.

He blushed. "Barbara wants your baby. I just want you."

Len knew all along. Maybe they had waited here together, making big plans for the Shaw sisters and how they could use their lives as a way to take care of their own unfinished business.

I pushed myself away from him. "I am not yours to take. You are not protecting me. You are making this worse."

Len wet his lips anxiously. "I protected you by being here today, and doesn't that mean anything to you? What did you think was going to happen just now? She wasn't going to let you live! She was going to burn you up from the inside out."

I shuddered. "So, I owe you what now?"

His pupils were huge as he took me in. "That should be easy to figure out."

Len crawled over to where I was sitting, his fingers grazed my bare thigh. I tried to jerk my nightgown down, and he fought me, diving into my neck and leaving scorching kisses behind.

"Stop," I said.

My skin crawled, and I was losing grip on this reality.

I was wrong about everyone I thought had been taking care of me as a kid. I thought Barbara was my friend. But she took our conversations as a way to learn how to edge herself into my mind for whatever reason she needed a second chance for. I thought Len was my first love, but he had groomed me mercilessly and left me confused and scarred. I hurt my family because of how these spirts treated me.

I refused to let this leak over to my child. I refused to let this be my life after I had worked so hard to change into someone else.

"No!" I screamed, putting my hand up and focusing all of my energy into a ball I saw as staticky yellow light.

Len jerked back three feet, shocked.

"I said no. I don't owe you anything. I can't help you anymore. Please leave."

He looked like he was capable of strangling me without a second thought, but I kept up that field of electricity. It filled me up with power and control. Eventually, he stood and walked out of the living room. I collapsed, holding onto my stomach and promising myself that I would be who I needed to be for this baby.

I would never allow Barbara to hurt them. I would never allow her to control my body in a way that could take this beautiful gift from me. And I would never let Len touch me again, period.

*

"I am just not sure this is what we need to be doing? This chick tried to kill my future nephew. Will this really keep her away?" Macy asked, sweeping smoldering sage around the living room at Missy's instruction.

"Nephew?" Missy asked, raising her brows at me.

I shrugged. "Macy thinks that she can project whatever gender she prefers onto my child just through *positive reinforcement.*"

Terry chuckled and moved into the kitchen and dining room.

"Yes, this will help. I don't know how strong Barbara is, but I do know that this will buy us some time to work on your mind's defenses, so you can guard yourself against any future attacks."

I sank onto the couch, the smell of sage giving me a headache. A future attack? How was one not enough? I was at my emotional and physical breaking point. Pregnancy was supposed to be full of joyful anticipation, not an internal apocalypse. Nothing was turning out the way it was supposed to.

Macy squeezed my shoulder and went to sage Mom's room. I took a deep breath and headed into the sunroom to grab my book. A long, warm bath was just what I needed. My skin prickled as I realized someone was watching me from the porch.

Barbara stood on the other end of the glass; her expression completely dead. In her anger, her image flickered back and forth between who she tried to show me and the shadow figure that had latched themselves with her.

They acted as leeches, draining energy and life from that half-world. Her anger gave them more power, and she sent them out like insurgents to do her will. She ran her nails across the glass, emitting a screech that spiked through my mind.

I put my hands over my ears, wanting to push her away. But I was utterly drained from my experience with her earlier.

"Go away!" I yelled. The projection reached behind me instead, aiming to merge with whatever spiritual energy could help me.

"That's her," Terry whispered from behind me.

I jumped, not realizing she had joined me.

"What?"

Terry pointed to Barbara, able to see her through my calling projection.

"That's her, who I see in the mirror when I go into my past self. It's me."

*

"Where do we start?" Ash asked, pulling her laptop onto a couch pillow on her crossed legs.

She didn't trust Barbara and was convinced that she had tricked her way into our home. I didn't want to investigate her, but Terry recognizing her and realizing she was also the culprit of all of Terry's pain made it impossible not to.

"I am not sure. She has kept her death state hidden for the most part, I don't know for sure how it happened. It's not something you can really ask someone."

"What did the pieces of it look like?"

I took a grounding breath and tried to remember. Terry was excited when she found out that Barbara was my spirit guide. She asked me a million questions. Terry seemed to think it was further proof of it being meant to be. But I was left feeling desperate and dirty for having another line of thought.

"Speckles of blood on her head and shoulders. There wasn't a ton of trauma that was visible from the front."

"Maybe a car accident? If the trauma was internal, you might not have seen it."

Seeing me go pale she stiffened.

"I am so sorry Claire. Of course, you don't want to research car accidents."

I shook the residual sound of breaking glass from my ears. "No, it's okay. I agree. If it were something as obvious as a drowning, I would have noticed it already."

Ash nodded and began her Google search. After a couple of minutes, she bit her lower lip and shrugged.

"Nothing. No accidents on this street. We don't know her last name, it's hard to just search for women between the ages of 20 and 30 who might have died in a car accident. Just because she lived next door doesn't mean she died here."

"Any deaths at all in the house next door?" I asked, looking over her shoulder.

"Other than an elderly man who had a stroke in his 80s, no. Whatever happened, she's keeping it close to her vest. She must have just come back here because it's where she lived, where she is tethered."

I sighed. "That might be why she came to me. No one else in our house has the ability to see or hear her. She is definitely not a spirit guide. But how am I supposed to know? There's not exactly a human resource number I can call. What if she is my guide and I push her away? I will never learn to put up boundaries and spirits will just bother me whenever they want."

She laid back on the couch pillows. "I don't know Claire. If she was the right guide for you, would we feel the need to do this?"

She gestured to her computer screen and the fact that we were hiding from Terry to search. In her excitement, she had utterly ignored why we were smudging the house in the first place.

"I guess not."

I knew in my heart that Barbara was latched onto our family because she needed us to act out her final chapter. Despite that, I still had no idea who she was or what steps to take next to protect my family.

*

Holden handed me a box of string lights with a discouraging look.

"What's wrong? Do you think we need more?" I asked, standing back to analyze the tree that he had brought over from the live tree lot.

"No, it's just, if this is Terry's past life, do we have to be wary of her as well? How far does this merging of them go? What if she tries to hurt the baby as well?"

I looked at the garlands instead of him. I wanted to yell at him for even asking me that. But it was the first thing to come to mind when Terry had told me that she recognized Barbara.

Being connected to someone with that many shadow figures attached to her could only hurt Terry. Not only was Barbara able to influence me and enter me in a way, but she had also been slowly gaining Terry's trust and working within her for months. What did that mean?

Macy was super freaked out and I needed a break from all of this. When Holden came over with the tree, Macy asked Terry to go shopping with her for a Christmas present for Britney. She and Brit were going through a rough patch, and she needed help. But I think she also felt better knowing that Terry wasn't under the same roof as me.

"I want to say no, that she isn't capable of hurting the baby or me," I said finally, dropping to my butt and scooching closer to the tree.

"But you don't really know."

I shrugged, I tried to act casual but my throat was thick, and my nose was running.

"I am sorry, I didn't mean to make you cry," Holden said, sitting next to me.

"No, it's not just this. I get that this scares you. But I just feel like a mess right now and have no control over my feelings. Or my vomit. Or my nose, apparently," I wiped my face with the corner of my shirt.

The corner of Holden's mouth quirked up. "I don't mind."

"You don't mind?" I asked, laughing.

He leaned forward and laid his hand on my belly; it was rounder in the last week and really starting to become noticeable. I wasn't feeling movement yet, but my doctor told me to expect the first flutters any day. I craved that reassurance more than I ever thought possible. I needed to hear from this little one, to know they were healthy and safe.

"It's insane, you know? How much I love this baby already, how much it makes me love you."

I looked at my belly, where our child slept. "It's more than before?"

Holden sighed, trying to put his thoughts into words.

"Well, yeah. Because it's not just us anymore. I love you as Claire, I have since I was 15. But now, I love you as the mother of my child. It's much deeper than just our connection. I look forward to loving you because of how you love them."

My nose dripped precariously again. "You're not really helping this situation right now."

"Can I help?" he asked, giving me a playful eyebrow.

Holden had been so great these last couple months, giving me space but still making it clear that he was in this with me 100%. I wanted all of him, all of us. But I still needed to heal with my sisters to be able to raise my baby in a family that wasn't carrying baggage from our past.

I needed to be able to go into this relationship without my parents' marriage hanging over my head. I hated feeling like I was leading him on, letting him believe that I was ready for full commitment before I really was.

"I don't know, things are still kind of crazy," I started, having to physically lean back because I was having to restrain myself from burying my fingers in his hair.

He pulled me back. "Claire, I know. I am not asking you to say yes to marrying me right now or letting me stay forever. But I love you, we are doing this together. Just let me stay the night, especially after all of this."

I looked at him, the openness and just genuine kindness that was in his heart. "You didn't say anything about sleeping."

Holden gaze twinkled. "Neither did you."

He kissed me first, but I let my body take control. I had missed him so much. I was ravenous to have us connected again, to be able to share this pain with him. This love. I paused before he removed my shirt, suddenly self-conscious of how much my body had changed. He laced our fingers together where they had stilled over the waistband of my maternity jeans.

"Claire, there is no you that I don't want. You were pretty back in high school, you were gorgeous last summer, and you are perfection now."

It was just as intense as that night in the mountains, in the water where we had skinny dipped for the first time. The Christmas lights danced over our skin, and the fire blazing in the fireplace kept us warm. I kissed him over and over, telling him I loved him and giving him all that I had inside of me over the last four months of missing him.

"I love you," I breathed into his mouth.

He buried his face in my chest, and I looked over his shoulder, where a shadow seemed to be blocking the light left on in the dining room. I froze as I realized it was Len, watching us make love.

His eyes danced with rage but his hand worked over himself as if it was him with me instead of Holden. Bile rose in my throat as a million memories of pain at his hands filled my mind. It edged into my heart and combined with Holden in a way that threatened to poison what we had.

"What's wrong," he asked as I abruptly rolled over and began dry heaving in panic, wanting to purge myself of all that Len had done to me.

I sat up, pointing to the dining room. The doorway was now empty, but I still smelled the cologne that Len had always worn. I still felt him on me.

Terry

I wanted to find out who Barbara was, who I was, but looking with Claire made me feel incredibly conflicted. I loved my sister; I have spent my entire life taking care of her and doing my best to make sure she was safe and cared for.

I loved this baby already and knew that it was going to be a beautiful chapter in our family's lives. I was so anxious for them to join our family and to become an aunt. Knowing what Barbara did to her over the last few months, I was terrified of what the spirit version of Barbara had in mind.

But as scared as Claire was, I refused to believe that she was all bad because she was also a part of me. Claire saying Barbara was evil or a negative ghost killed a piece of me. Maybe who I became in my visions of the past and the spirit Barbara were separate entities altogether. A broken part that needed to be reunited with her one true love to become whole and full of light again. Maybe I could save Claire by allowing Barbara to find love again.

As we searched for photos and information online, I came across Eli's profile again. I heard Claire calling me, pointing to areas on my computer screen, but I was fading away into another vision. Into Barbara and who I was before I became a Shaw.

"Okay, I'll call you tomorrow?" Kerry said, sitting up and kissing my bare shoulder.

I sighed and turned away from him. "Sure."

"What's wrong? Aren't you excited? Isn't this what you wanted?" he asked, his eyebrows knitting.

"You know that it is. Which is exactly why it's not really going to happen. You are going to go home, you are going to find a reason to put it off, and you are going to call me tomorrow to set up a booty call."

"B, stop."

I tasted anger like bile creeping up my throat. "Tell me this is different."

Kerry dropped down in front of me and kissed me. "Please, just trust me. Just this once more."

I kissed him goodbye, knowing this was different. It felt like a final goodbye. My life was changing for good or for bad. The air was very still, and my nerves jumped crazily. Eventually, I took a bath and cried myself to sleep. I was going to wake up tomorrow and my whole relationship with Kerry would be nothing but a memory. It was time to move on.

A knock woke me up around 4 am. I was afraid to open the door for some reason. I was scared of what kind of omens fate brings you in the middle of the night.

But it was fate bringing me Kerry. He was disheveled and carrying two duffel bags, but he was here. He was finally mine.

"Ter?!"

Claire's frightened face swam in front of me. She was holding onto my shoulders and shaking me.

"Stop, I'm back," I gurgled.

"That was super creepy. Were you just her? Do you just disappear like that? Your head fell back, and you just stared into nothingness."

I sat up, my head throbbing. "I'm sorry I scared you, but I saw something. Kerry left his wife for Barbara; it was what she wanted more than anything. She loved him, and their love was powerful. I just know it's why we are being brought back together."

Claire looked unsure but nodded. "Ter, that can't be the whole story. Because she is broken. She is here, and she is trying to finish whatever she left behind."

"Whatever happened didn't happen here, you said that yourself. Maybe that one change is enough to make things different for Eli and me. Maybe it's enough to let us write a new chapter where things end differently, and we get to be together."

"And you are willing to take that chance?" Claire asked, her cheeks reddening.

I looked at my feet, ready to come completely clean. "I wrote to Eli. He is coming to visit before summer starts. To figure out what this whole thing is and how it connects to the both of us. Maybe that's why she is angry, she has been separated from the man she loves for who knows how many years."

"Maybe. It could make things better. But there's a chance that connecting him and Barbara is the last thing we should do. What if that's who she is mad at? Seeing him might cause her to lose it completely, to force her to really hurt someone. It might not be you or Eli, it might be me."

My hand jumped up, meaning to slap Claire. I have never hit my sister in my entire life, I felt like I was losing my mind to this anger. But she could never understand what I was going through.

Eli is what I wanted more than anything in the world. Why was she begrudging me that? She had all that she could possibly want from life. A baby, a man that loved her, a career that she wasn't afraid of. Why did she want to take this one thing from me? I held my arms behind my back and took what I hoped was a steadying breath.

"Just trust me, please. Just this once."

Claire agreed, but she wrapped herself in her arms like an armored vest while nodding. She was distancing herself from me, believing that I was choosing this relationship over her. Maybe I was.

*

"Terry, I am not going away. Come on."

Claire had been knocking for the past 10 minutes. She refused to take the hint. For the most part, my sisters allowed me my 'dark days.' But every day seemed to be a dark day, and their patience seemed to be running out.

Last night I had asked Claire to come with me to see my mom's plot. She had agreed even though it was clear that she wanted nothing to do with that kind of scene. But when I woke up this morning, I had nothing left inside of me. It was hard to even motivate myself to put on deodorant.

I glared as Claire pushed herself into my room. She was holding sheets and wrinkling her nose.

"Hey," she said, from the doorway.

"Hey," I said, avoiding her questioning gaze.

"I get it if you're not up to going out today. But... your room stinks, and it's kind of escaping into the rest of the house. Please just get up for five minutes so I can change your sheets."

I looked at the clean green sheets in her arms and was flooded with shame. This is what I had become. The shut-in that didn't bathe or clean their room. I was living with my own body odor and dirty plates every single day, thinking it was what I deserved.

I saw it around me and had enough dignity to be embarrassed. But I didn't seem to know how to climb out of this hole either. At the very least, I climbed out of bed and stood next to it.

Claire balled up my sheets and threw them out into the hall next to the laundry room.

"I am still going to see Mom today. I am leaving in about a half hour. If you want to shower and come, now is a good time."

She wasn't grilling me, and she wasn't pressuring me, but I got the picture. I had been putting this off enough. I nodded and headed upstairs to shower while she finished and stole as many dirty clothes from my room that she could fit in her arms. I let myself be taken along, and in a half hour, we were at the graveyard.

This slab of marble didn't feel like something my mom wanted for herself. In fact, I couldn't picture her wanting a plot at all.

The girls didn't know. But it was still wrong and made a dull anger roll around in the pit of my stomach.

"Are you okay?" Claire asked, sitting on the ground, her little belly resting on top of her lap.

I sighed, breathing in the damp soil and leaves that were beginning to mildew. I sat next to her and gently dusted the dirt off of my mom's name.

"I think so. I don't feel… anything. Like she's not here."

She nodded. "I feel the same way. I kept waiting to be able to talk to her here and grieve in a way that gave me closure. It feels like she is still very much a part of this world. I feel like it makes it harder to move on."

Once again, a stab of jealousy hit me whenever I thought of Claire's gift making it easier for her to connect with the mom she didn't want when she was here.

But she really had changed over the summer. Macy kept trying to convince me that Claire was a completely different person. She said that Claire pulled through for her after the accident. That was incredibly hard for me to imagine, yet here she was.

Being the first person to come to the graveyard with me, making dinner on days when it was impossible to pull myself out of bed, helping Macy with her homework and being there to listen. She let me hate her in silence when I was having a bad day and taking my grief out on her. She was growing up into someone that Mom would be proud of. That broke my heart most of all.

I hated the idea of this slab with my mother's name on it, but I did have to admit that it was beautiful. Claire had done a great job of picking one out. Not for the first time, I wished they had taken photos of the service so that I didn't have to imagine the whole thing in my head. I didn't want to attend my mom's funeral but wasn't able to deny the loss of closure that I still felt.

"We played Unchained Melody," Claire said softly, seeming to read my mind.

My face fell. "You know, Mom never really intended to have this big burial. She wanted some of her ashes to be sprinkled at the beach and for us to take a trip together in memory of her."

Claire blushed. "I know, she left a little note in her insurance wishes. I kept some of the ashes, and we buried the rest. They are in a safety deposit box at the funeral home. We didn't want to do it without you. We hated the idea of having them at home if you weren't. Then, when you were back, I didn't know how to bring it up."

My stomach dropped. All of this time I had been sure she hadn't done well by our mother. But she was just afraid of me freaking out if she tried to take the initiative she had been showing all summer.

"What did she write?" I asked her.

"Just that she wanted some of her ashes to be spread in Long Beach. It looked like she meant to write more and was distracted."

I nodded. "We talked about it a few times, after a hard day at work and she was all reflective about time. She wanted us to take a trip to the beach together, just the three of us. To spend the weekend thinking of her and being together, then spread her ashes at the beach."

Claire's cried silently, turning from me. I knew she was thinking of and regretting the last beach trip we tried to plan.

"What if we did it now, go to the beach?" I told her, putting my arm around her shoulder. "It's not too late."

*

Macy had been asking for a lot of alone time, but it wasn't right to ignore her crying in her room for yet another night.

"Mac?" I said, pushing the door open.

She sat up quickly and tried wiping the tears from her cheeks.

"Stop, I already heard you. Do you want to talk about it?"

She shook her head.

"Mac, I don't want to push you, but this is getting worse. You are crying all the time, and I know something happened. You have to talk to me."

I sat on the bed, and she took a deep breath.

"Shayla is getting worse. She looks terrible, not showering and jumping every time someone slams a locker shut. She was falling apart, so I confronted Simon."

"And?"

Macy cried harder and gently touched my arm. She didn't want to tell me, but she could show me. I wanted to rip my arm away but had to do this for my sister. I might still be able to protect her.

"Simon!" Macy yelled.

She half ran over to the locker room where Simon was coming out with his hair still damp from the gym.

His face broke into a smile, and he looked completely harmless. The captain of the poetry club and writer of a love poem that won a national award last year.

"Don't look at me like that. We aren't friends. Shayla isn't talking to anyone, and I won't let you get away with this. You took advantage of her, and you need to make it right."

He laughed, and she became aware of how very alone they were. Everyone was in class, and the hallway by the gym was deserted. She was alone and wrong about him being a good guy.

"I need to make it right? What happens if I don't?" he asked, stepping closer.

Macy tried to back up. Simon pressed her against the lockers, covering her mouth with his mouth when she tried to scream. She was so shocked she didn't even fight him.

"I am tired of girls pretending like they don't want exactly what I want. You know, I heard you and Britney were dating. Maybe you just haven't met the right guy yet, maybe you haven't been touched the right way yet," his breath was hot and disgusting on her neck.

Macy started crying, and he slid his hand up her shirt, touching her breast. Then he knocked her against the lockers once more and left her in the hallway alone.

Macy released my arm and collapsed into loud sobs.

"Mac, did you tell anyone?" I asked, feeling sick with guilt.

"No, I wanted to tell Britney. To tell Shayla. But it was my fault. I had put her in the same situation and then went alone

175

to talk to him. I hate this gift; I get why Claire didn't want one. If Claire didn't see spirits, then she would have never met Len in the first place. If I didn't see these stupid auras, I wouldn't have set up Shayla, or fought with Britney, and Simon wouldn't have hurt me."

"Macy no, this wasn't because of your vision. This is because of Simon."

She pushed me away. "No, Ter. It's not just their fault. It wasn't just Lens fault. Why did Mom tell us that being this way made us special? All it brings us is pain."

I gripped her arms, and she yelped. Her crying slowed, and she looked at me with a deeply creased brow.

"It is their fault. No one ever deserves to be hurt. They don't deserve pain for feeling lost, for being alone, or for trusting another person. We don't belong to anyone but ourselves and do not deserve to be touched like that. Not ever. It's not Claire's fault, and it's not your fault."

She searched my face, and I saw a tiny part of her forgiving herself, finally. She let go of wanting to blame our gifts.

"Putting the blame somewhere else makes it easier not to tell, but that protects the people who do these kinds of things. You have to be strong, Mac. I will help you. I will keep you safe."

Macy nodded. "Okay."

She wrapped her arms around my waist and cried into my chest. I stroked her hair and promised to keep her safe. My family would never hurt this way again.

*

I thought that getting through to Macy would have made me feel stronger, but I was still drowning. After going to the graveyard the day before, the blackness seemed darker than ever. While counseling myself to sleep, I had gripped my wine bottle and thought of how easy it might be to escape altogether. I could take the rest of the painkillers from the hospital in one gulp and be gone by morning.

As soon as I contemplated leaving, my mouth filled with gunpowder. I choked over and over, spitting to get the acrid taste out of my mouth. I heard Barbara laughing and knew I was beginning to follow her path right down to her death.

It scared me so much that I got out of bed. I took another shower, spitting all the gunpowder down the drain. I threw away all the wine in the fridge, and I cleaned my room for the first time since coming home. I was able to clear the garbage and pain away at the same time. It made me feel stronger.

I might not have been able to go back to work yet, but I might be able to still use those skills to help Macy. I could still make a difference if I kept holding on.

Chapter 8

Claire

December 2015

"It's a big deal, I promise you. You laugh now, but every year you will look for yours," I told Holden.

I gave him a paint pen to write his name on the glass ornaments that made up most of our decorations.

"Is this a good spot?" Holden asked, pointing to the side facing the sunroom.

"Absolutely," Macy said, moving hers towards the front.

I laughed; Holden had to figure the rest of it out on his own. Doing this together felt like taking such a big step. Seeing his ornament on our tree seemed more permanent than getting tattoos together or wearing matching gold rings. I stepped back, the pine smell of the tree suddenly overwhelming.

"Claire, please. Stop!" Macy said, laying down and holding onto her stomach.

I had heard of sympathy pains during pregnancy, but I wondered if any other psychic had been able to project their symptoms onto their loved ones. Terry was craving huge glasses of cold milk even though she was lactose intolerant, Macy was suffering from ridiculous nausea and had been eating Saltines since this morning, and Holden's back was aching painfully. I was feeling all three of those things plus a heavy baby in my belly pushing my hip bones apart. Sharing the pain was helping more than I was letting on.

"I'm sorry," I chuckled, getting up to help Terry in the kitchen with Christmas dinner.

Today had been pretty perfect considering that it was our first Christmas without Mom. Our tree was beautiful, dinner smelled terrific, and we had been able to set out Mom's decorations without bawling. Best of all, no ghosts. It was just the four of us.

"Do you need any help?" I asked Terry, who was nursing another glass of milk with a self-loathing expression.

"Take this from me," she said, clenching it at the same time.

I peeled her fingers off of the glass and looked into the pot where pasta was boiling lazily.

"Ham, mashed potatoes, mac and cheese, roasted carrots and broccoli, and fruit salad. Am I missing anything?" she asked, looking around the kitchen.

"Rolls?"

"Rolls," she agreed, she looked like she would rather stop the garbage disposal with her foot than go back to Walmart.

We had shopped yesterday, which was a terrible idea. Holden had practically had to commit assault for the last can of pumpkin.

"We're good," Holden said, grabbing a grocery bag from the table. He handed a bag of Hawaiian rolls to her.

Terry let out a breath and kissed him on the cheek. "Best brother ever."

Holden glowed, and I couldn't help but smile seeing how well he fit here with me. I didn't want it to be this easy to move on from our life with Mom. Everything that was different today seemed to put more distance between us and her memory.

But it was easy to see this house in my child's future and the other children that might fill our home someday. My child's first Thanksgiving dinner, hunting for eggs in the backyard, playing with the nativity scene when no one was looking.

As if staking their claim on this future, my child rolled gently in my stomach like a butterfly. I gasped and touched where the movement had been. A nudge caressed my palm, my little ones first high five.

Terry saw me holding my belly and lifted a brow in question. I reached for one of her hands and one of Holden's. I put them on my stomach. The baby gave a big roll, making each of them laugh.

"Mac! Hurry up! The baby's kicking!" Terry called out into the living room.

We heard a muffled retch, and then the bathroom door cracked. "Leave me alone! I will be the best aunt in the world, I promise. Just leave me alone."

I giggled. "Love you, Mac. I'm sorry."

She mumbled and retched again.

"Anyone hungry?" Terry asked, giving my belly a pat before grabbing plates.

Holden put his arm around me and kissed my cheek. "It's like holding my entire family. It's the best Christmas present in the world."

I leaned forward, surprising him with a small kiss on the lips.

"We are, your family I mean. This baby is lucky to have you as a dad."

He sat at the dining room table after pulling a chair out for me.

"Maybe after the holidays, we should revisit that conversation. About me moving in and making things official again. I don't want to put any pressure on you. I just don't want to miss things like this. I don't want to be left out."

I nodded. "Okay. After the holidays, let's go out and decide what the next step is."

He squeezed my knee under the table, and I knew that I would say yes. I was thankful for his place in my life and for the time to think about what future we had together. When I looked at Holden, it was easy to want to fall into forever. But that fall, it still terrified me.

*

"It doesn't seem silly to hang these up on the years it doesn't even snow?" Holden asked, balancing on a ladder and leaning to untack the Christmas lights on the porch he had hung the month before.

"No! The weather doesn't dictate our holiday spirit," Terry said, cradling a pumpkin spice latte.

New Year's Eve was tomorrow, and she was squeezing as much Christmas goodness as possible into the rest of December. She was even wearing Mom's old Christmas sweaters despite it being close to 60 degrees out here.

"Stop being a Grinch," Macy said, hugging the plastic Santa on the lawn that she had picked out when she was five.

Holden leaned forward; his back revealed under his shirt as he stretched more than the ladder was allowing him to. I wanted to call out to him, but before the words left my mouth, I saw a black wisp blast through the yard. Macy screamed, seeing it as well. Holden was suspended in the air for a moment then hit the walkway with a wet smack. He turned a sickly gray color, and his forehead glistened with sweat.

"Holden!"

His arm was already swelling, and he held it against his body.

"Where does it hurt?!" Terry asked, grabbing various body parts while he tried to wriggle away from her.

"My arm. I think it's broken."

"Should we call an ambulance?" Macy asked, flushing and then going pale again. She looked like she was ready to pass out.

"No!" Holden choked out.

"Babe, your arm. We need to call 911," I told him, placing his head in my lap and brushing his hair off his face.

"I know, I know. But I don't have health insurance right now. My dad can't afford anything more… it was too expensive. I can't be paying for an ambulance for the rest of my life. But I do need a ride to the ER."

I nodded and ran trembling fingers through his hair, resting on his cheek. Even in this kind of agony, he was still thinking of his family. Practical to a fault.

We helped him up and folded him into the front of Terry's car. Macy hugged me and went around to the driver's seat.

"It's okay. We will get him fixed up," she told me.

I leaned into the door and kissed Holden on the cheek before getting into the backseat.

"I am so sorry."

"I guess that's what being a Grinch will get me. I will be more careful next time," he said, forcing a chuckle.

I wanted to smile at him, but I am sure it was more like a grimace. Maybe he didn't see the shadow figures, but Macy and I had. Was being here safe for him? We had talked about being ready to move in together, but now I wasn't sure. I wasn't sure it was okay for him to be here when the shadow figures saw him as a threat. I wasn't able to outrun the ghosts and might never be safe.

*

Soft hands caressed my arms, pinning me to the bed in one gentle stroke. I sighed, kisses trailing up my shoulder and my neck. Lips pressed against mine, my tongue meeting theirs with eagerness.

As I wrapped my arms around him, the last couple of days returned to me. Holden's arm being broken and Ash coming over to keep me company. Ash being in my room, in the bed next to me. My eyes snapped open. Len was poised above me. I tried to scream and push him away.

His mouth sealed our kiss, not letting any sound escape. I thrashed, and his fingers dug into my arms. I felt him going further than just my lips, his darkness stealing down my throat and filling my chest.

Going into my throat, finding its way to my womb. Fear filled my body as his fingers groped for my child, wanting to destroy the product of my relationship with Holden. Maybe he believed that if he hurt my child, he would remove the wall between us. That it was the last thing separating us.

Ash rolled over and cracked one eye. With a scream, she sat up and stumbled off the edge of the bed.

"Claire!" she shrieked.

I wondered how much she saw, how much I was projecting in pure panic. I reached for her, still struggling underneath Len. She extended her hand and gripped mine in return. I centered myself from inside and pushed him away, drawing all of the strength from Ash that I possibly could.

Finally, he was ripped from me, and I took a breath. I wanted to vomit. To dispel his touch in one action and be able to dispose of him forever. I held my stomach, my child rolled enthusiastically under my hands.

Ash collapsed onto the bed next to me, staring at where Len stood on the other side of the room in complete fear.

"How could you?" I said, my voice raw from emotion.

Len glared at me. "If that baby was gone, what would keep you from leaving him?"

"I don't love you. This isn't love, you tricked me into being with you. Kissing me and touching me in that way, when I am fighting you off. You are taking away my choice, and that's the only way you will ever have me. I love Holden because he is the complete opposite of you," I spat at him.

Ash sat up and rubbed my back, shaking as she hugged me.

As Len processed my words, he paced around the room, grunting in anger and making the walls tremble. He turned to look at me one more time, he was able to turn me inside out with that one glare. He was able to see my most vulnerable pieces and expose them for the world to see. He held my gaze and tried pulling me into that darkness. I closed my eyes, breaking the connection. But I heard his roar of fury and glass grazed my cheeks as he destroyed the room.

Terry

December 2015

Shopping with Macy reminded me of shopping for Claire's birthday present last spring. It felt like a million years ago even though it hadn't even been a year. Macy had decided to go to the winter dance after all, with Shayla. She mostly wanted to go because she wanted to make sure Britney was just on the date to make her mad. I imagined all of the ways that she might be hurt by whatever she saw. But when she made up her mind, it was impossible to talk her out of going.

"What do you think of this?" I asked her, pulling out a black dress with lace on the neckline.

Macy shook her head. "I was thinking something more… slinky."

"Of course, you were," I said, laughing a little bit.

She took a dramatic breath and continued shopping. "Shayla decided to talk to the counselor. I promised her that I will tell them what happened if she came clean. I don't know what is going to happen to Simon, but it's better than him just walking around like nothing happened."

"What did they tell her?" I asked.

"Well, basically, since what happened wasn't on school property, they have to report it to the police. Their one option is to suspend him if she presses charges or asks for a restraining order."

My skin prickled painfully, I still felt so guilty for what had happened to Macy. I hated the idea of her going to school every day and having to see him.

"That's hard. She is going to have to go through things in detail and decide whether or not she wants to face him in court. A lot of victims decide it isn't worth having to go through it in public like that."

"I know. She's terrified. She's taking the weekend to talk to her parents and decide what to do. They found out the night it happened but weren't able to force her to go to the police. I think they will be happy to find out that the school is on their side on the whole thing. They want him to be punished."

I knew from experience that it was hard to find justice in these situations, but Macy didn't need to hear that right now. She needed to stay focused on each step between now and whatever happened next. Her process of finding peace might be completely different than Shayla's.

"But what happened to you was on school property," I reminded her.

Macy nodded. "I know. I am going to tell, I have to. But I want you and Claire to come with me."

I stopped, turning to look at her. Claire didn't know what had happened yet. Under normal circumstances, we would have told Dad, but things were still terrible between him and Macy. He didn't make her feel safe, and he might even blame her for part of it. Simon saying that he was helping her figure out if she was gay was too much for her to have to admit to him after what they went through last year.

We had wanted to tell Claire, but it was hard with her pregnancy. We didn't want to make her anymore stressed than she already was. But waiting this long probably hadn't been a great idea either. She was going to feel betrayed and have to process her feeling over the sexual assault in light of her own situation.

"I don't want to hurt her, but I need her there with me," Macy said, apparently seeing my turmoil.

"I wish I could have kept you both from being hurt in the first place," I told her.

Macy nodded firmly, accepting it but also accepting that it wasn't the way things turned out. As she slowly scrutinized the racks, her face lit up. She grabbed a bright purple dress from behind me. It had a sheer panel on the sides and a low back.

"I think this is perfect."

I watched her live her life despite all of the things that were crazy right now. Macy had a way of compartmentalizing that made ordinary seem possible again. It reassured me that life went on.

"I do, too."

*

Backstreet Boys always improved my mood, and I was having an off day. I ruined my eggs; I was bloated from too much salt last night and got nail polish on the couch while doing my nails this morning. I was attempting to cook again, this time an omelet, and gave myself a soundtrack. I danced around the kitchen, wiping off the counters as I went and planning dinner for that night.

"I want it that way," I sang into the spatula.

I heard the back door open and turned around in a dramatic sweep, meaning to make Macy laugh. I jumped and dropped the spatula when I saw it was CJ instead.

"Oh, hi," I said, touching the frazzled ponytail I had wrestled my hair into.

His lips twitched, making them look incredibly kissable. The thought made me blush, making it even more uncomfortable in this room that was already too small. We hadn't really talked since his birthday, and it was our first time seeing each other. I knew that he meant that night to be a new beginning for us, the last beginning really. I didn't know how to move on from it.

"Hi," he said, holding up a paper bag.

He walked across the kitchen and gave me a stiff peck me on the cheek. He always kissed me on the cheek, but this was the first time I remember it feeling formal as if I were his great aunt. CJ placed the paper bag in front of me and took out the ice cream it held. A pint of Cherry Garcia, my favorite. CJ knowing me so well didn't really make this any easier.

"Thank you," I said, going to the freezer to put it away.

"Yeah, no problem. I just thought… ice cream felt like a good peace offering."

CJ sat at the kitchen table, and I finished my omelet.

"Are you hungry?" I asked.

He shook his head, and I joined him at the table for my lunch.

"How have you been?" he asked.

I shrugged. "Fine. I am finally getting through some paperwork for the center. Getting up to date on my old patients."

"How does it feel? Are you planning on going back?"

"I want to… but there's a lot of baggage there for me. Sometimes I wish that I was able to just start over somewhere new. In a center where they don't know that I failed Gina."

CJ leaned over and gently squeezed my hand. "You didn't fail. You see the past. I doubt that even Gina really knew what was going to happen. She reached her breaking point and made a disgusting choice."

I nodded, but it didn't make me feel any better. I was working with my mom last year. She saw the future and was still unable to really see what was unfolding in front of us. The truth is that Gina tricked us. I wanted to believe that I was helping her so much that I failed to do my job. I let her get away with hurting her mom, and my sisters were tricked into helping her commit murder. Lucas was a psycho, but Gina was a monster.

"What about you? What have you been up to?" I asked, going back to my food.

"Just working… It's been hard getting back into a routine. Us not talking makes things really weird. It makes it hard to just pretend like things are normal."

CJ blushed, and I knew that this was hard for him to talk about. He had made himself vulnerable over and over, wishing things were different. I wanted him to be happy, but this was the first time I had chosen myself over someone else's feelings. This was important.

"I'm sorry. I didn't mean for that night to end that way," I said, unsure of how much to give him.

A huge part of me wanted to reach out and hold him. But if I did that, how much of this plan for my future would unravel?

"You didn't?" CJ asked, he crossed his arms over his chest and I sensed the distance he placed between us to protect himself.

"No, I never wanted to hurt you. But I am going to see where this goes. With Eli."

He sat back, his cheeks reddening. "Eli? The guy from California?"

I nodded. "I am sorry, but he's not just some guy. I wish I were able to explain it better. He's important, he is who my old soul is connected to. I have to see where this goes or I will always wonder. In our past life, he gave up his whole life to be with me."

"His whole life? Wait... was he married?" CJ asked, his mouth fell open in disgusted disbelief.

I blushed and tried to look away. "What does that have to do with anything? He met me and fell in love with me. That could not have happened if they were meant to be."

"Do you even hear yourself? The Terry I know would have never trusted a man who betrayed the woman they were committed to. Don't you see how empty that it? I would never do that to you, you were always my first choice."

I shook my head. "Maybe I am not the Terry you know anymore."

CJ half stood without looking away from me. "Do you love him?"

I wanted to hold his eyes and answer with naked honesty, but it was impossible. I couldn't just agree because he knew me well enough to see through it if it wasn't the whole truth.

I did love Eli, but part of me also loved CJ. The part of my soul that lived in the past wasn't able to imagine a life without Eli, but the part of me that belonged to this world was meant to love CJ. I couldn't have one without the other, but I had to know.

"I do," I said finally.

CJ nodded, came over to my side of the table to kiss me on the head, then left. I waited until he was gone before letting myself cry. There were no winners here. It didn't matter who I ended up with, a part of my heart would always be unsatisfied. A piece of me would always be broken.

*

"I wonder why she kept these. She didn't want to have any more kids. She didn't even want to date," Macy said, holding up a dusty onesie.

We were going through the attic where Mom had kept trunks of mementos, from our baby clothes to our old school dance dresses zipped up in plastic bags. Claire wanted to keep as much of it as possible, even though she was refusing to tell us whether or not she had any inklings of what the gender of the baby was.

"For this reason? For us to be able to go through it and remember. To be able to wrap our kids in these memories," Claire said softly, touching the onesie she was holding with reverence.

She was usually not a sentimental person, so her frequent emotional outbursts and tears were still very strange to us. I always had to pretend like I didn't see because making it a big deal just made her more upset. She sniffled and turned, pretending to look at the box behind her. Macy bit her lips together to keep from giggling.

"Is all of this ours?" I asked, standing up to look at a necklace I saw hanging from the mirror propped against one wall.

I recognized it before I came to it, a pearl hanging from a delicate strand of white gold. Goosebumps broke out across from arms as I reached to it. As my fingers brushed the cold metal, I fell into the memories that Barbara had left for me.

"I don't understand, did I do something wrong?" I asked, clutching Kerry's clothes to my chest so that he couldn't shove them into the duffel bag sitting on my bed.

Not just my bed, our bed. The one we had shared for the last three months. Life had been perfect. Him going off to work when I did, coming back home and having dinner together. Falling asleep together and having date nights out on the town like we were never able to before. It was perfect.

So why was he leaving now?

Kerry gently unraveled my fingers and took the clothes from me, folding his shirts into neat squares even though he was shaking.

"Kerry! Look at me," I shrieked, hating how thin and desperate my voice sounded.

He turned slowly, tears running down his face. I caressed his cheek, and he leaned into my touch.

"If this is what you want, why are you like this? Stay with me. Whatever it is, we will figure it out," I whispered, wrapping my arms around him to reach his lips.

Kerry stepped back. "Barb, I wish... I wish it were that easy. But I fucked up. This is bigger than just you and me. It's Rachel."

I prickled like he had shocked me. Kerry was mine now, but her name was still a forbidden word in this house. The name that had the power to shatter the dream I had been living in. A name that still had some influence over the man I loved.

"What about her?" I said, anger beginning to fill my stomach and clotting my vision with black spots.

He sat on the bed, he looked utterly defeated.

"She… she came to my office yesterday. She's pregnant."

I sank to my knees, feeling like the ground was opening up to swallow me whole.

"How do you know she really is? This might be her getting back at you for leaving," I said, my words tearing at my throat.

"She brought the ultrasound, Barbara. She is twelve weeks along. She plans on keeping the baby."

The whites of his eyes were red and looked raw. I knew that his father had left their family when he was young and that having a second chance at being a dad was one of the things, he wanted most in his life. But those children were supposed to be our children. It was supposed to be our life. I had given him three years and made so many sacrifices. Even though I hated myself, I had to ask him to make this sacrifice for me.

"That's it? We won't fight to make this work. You can see the baby on weekends, or we could adopt it ourselves. We could still do this… together. "I said, choking with tears.

Kerry stood up and zipped his duffel bag. He turned and looked at me, resolute in his decision.

"Leaving you will be something that kills me every single day, but I won't be able to live with myself if I left my child. I will not be my dad."

"But I can't live with myself if you leave," I whispered.

He walked towards me like he wanted to kiss me one last time and I almost let him. Instead, my hand shot up on its own accord, and I slapped him. The sting in my palm was satisfying, but once he was gone, I regretted that being the last expression I saw on his face.

I laid on the ground, unable to move and let myself dissolve into panic and regret. I wanted to feel only sadness and emptiness, but I was becoming fuller by the minute. Filled with anger, pain, and bitter vengeance.

A clawing at my arms brought me back to the present, to the attic.

"Terry!" Macy's voice screamed in my ears.

She slapped me, and I rocked back into my own consciousness. I saw a lamp in my grip and let it drop, watching it shatter as if it was happening to someone else. Claire cowered in the corner across from me, staring at me with fearful anger.

Macy pushed me back gently. "Are you back?"

I nodded, feeling like my mouth was full of mud. I spat red and realized it was blood.

"Did you hit me?" I asked Macy, frustrated with these moments that I came into myself with half a scene in my mind and half a scene in front of me.

When I left this body, it seemed like time stopped, but I guess that wasn't true.

"Yes!" Macy said, still holding onto my shoulders like she had to protect Claire from me. It made my stomach churn, but I wasn't able to feel apologetic about something I didn't remember doing.

"Why? What happened?"

"You swung that lamp at Claire. You had this insane look on your face and kept screaming that the baby was ruining your life. You tried to hurt her."

Claire blushed, unable to speak. My heart clenched, and I reached out to her. She pulled back and covered her stomach in a protective hug. I sank down, Macy still holding onto me.

"Not your baby, Claire. I was Barbara again... the man she loved, that we love, he left her because his wife was pregnant."

Macy's eyebrows raised. "He was married?"

I blushed, realizing I had withheld that for a long time because I was embarrassed by Barbara's transgressions. CJ's reaction had made me feel terrible, but that was nothing compared to the judgment in my sister's eyes.

"Yes, but he left her. We were living together, and then he left to be with her."

Claire paled. "Isn't that good? Doesn't that make him a good man for standing by his family?"

I stood up, my fists clenching. "I was his family. I still am."

I strode out of the attic with them watching me. It didn't make sense to them, I understood that. After how Dad left us, was it right to root for anyone walking out on their wife? Only I knew how it felt to be in Kerry's arms. They didn't know how I ached to be the one carrying a baby, guaranteeing his devotion to me forever. To carry a child that would make these dreams come true.

Instead, I was the odd one out. Instead, I was always empty.

Chapter 9

Claire

January 2016

In our haste to get Holden to the hospital, our plastic Santa was still standing lonely by our chain link fence. I bundled myself up and headed out to the yard, the grass crunching under my boots. We didn't have any snow yet, but the ground was still frozen and unforgiving beneath my feet.

"Hi," I heard from over the gate.

I straightened and saw a little boy, his light brown hair blowing in the frigid air. I saw that he wasn't wearing a coat and looked around for his parents.

"Hi, did you get lost out here?" I asked, coming to the gate.

He looked around. His lips trembled, and I sensed his fear. As he met my gaze again, I saw him flicker. My goosebumps weren't from the cold alone. He wasn't just lost, he was dead. I opened the gate and came out to kneel by him.

"My name is Claire. What's your name, buddy?"

He shifted, looking like a scared puppy. "I'm not supposed to talk to strangers."

I smiled. "That's good advice, but if you are lost, you might need help. Can I help you find your mommy and daddy?"

He shook his head. "We were at the lake."

I stood up. "Great. I'll take you there, and we can see if they are still around."

"They aren't. But he is."

"Who?" I asked, not wanting to look at him anymore. I tried to turn away from him but had to see this through.

"Him. I was alone there, and he became my friend. He just wanted one thing in return."

"What did he want?" I asked quietly.

"To touch me. He asked me to keep his secrets."

"He touched you? Who?" I kneeled down again and gasped as I saw him flicker again.

He might have been showing me the image of a little boy, but this spirit didn't belong in this body. It didn't belong in a shape this innocent. A mask came over the little boy's features, of Len laughing at me with hooded lids.

"He asked me to keep his secrets, but that's okay. I didn't mind being touched. I didn't want to pretend like I didn't like it."

I backed away. "Stop it. You're not him."

He laughed dropping his façade and letting his true face show through.

"No. I won't stop. I can touch anyone I want. I could touch you and any child who wanders too far at the lake. I can even touch them."

He pointed to my stomach, a sick smiled twisted over his features. I covered my belly as if to shield my child and shook my head furiously.

"You will never touch them or me ever again."

"How are you planning on stopping me? I've known Barbara for a long time, we waited for you together. She might have taught me a few tricks."

My mouth dropped open, but I had no response. I hadn't been able to protect myself, I had let myself become a victim. I was too wrapped up in myself to protect Macy, and she had gotten hurt. How was I going to protect my child?

I was wobbly as Len rushed towards me and filled my mind with a vision. I was wearing pink corduroy shorts, and grass was clenched in my fist.

"I don't think… someone will…."

Len gently squeezed my shoulder; I saw that his pants were hanging around his thighs and his erect penis was exposed.

"No one is going to come and get you into trouble. You're not doing anything wrong. You love me, right?"

I nodded frantically, not wanting him to abandon me too.

"When you love someone, this is how you show it. It's not a big deal."

I tried not to look down at his penis. What he wanted didn't make any sense to me. I was embarrassed and ashamed to be so lost on what to do. Len was older, he knew more about how

all of this worked. I felt like a dumb kid and didn't want him to
see me that way.

"My mouth?" I asked, scrunching my eyebrows.

"Yeah, not a big deal. I'll show you how...."

"Stop!" I screamed.

I forced my eyes open and pushed away from the vision. Len had learned more than just a few tricks from Barbara. He wasn't only strong enough to make me see his memories as my own, he was able to control my body like a puppet.

I had made my way over to the edge of our street and was inches away from the curb, where traffic continued just beyond it. I gasped and jumped back, running back to our yard. Len was gone, but I still felt his fingers from where they had dug into my arms and legs. He had planned on making me walk into traffic, killing me while trapping me in our shared past. If he couldn't have me, then no one else would either.

I sank to my knees, shaking and apologizing to my child. I had already broken my promise to protect my child over and over because of this lunacy. I was alone in the yard, crying with fresh grass stains on my jeans. I didn't feel relief knowing that he was gone. It wasn't forever, Len was only waiting for yet another weak moment.

*

I flipped through the pages that Ash had printed off the internet and shook my head.

"Is it bad?" I asked her.

She shrugged without commitment. "Will you read it anyway?"

Ash had come over as soon as she found Barbara's obituary. I should have been relieved that we finally had answers, but I was overwhelmed and unwilling. What did this change if they were going to attack my family and me regardless of what happened to them?

I read the first few pages and then sat down. "She didn't die here."

"Nope. She shot Kerry in his apartment and then committed suicide. He lived across town."

"Okay, I understand her being connected to her home. But what about Terry?" I asked her.

She sat across from me. "Do you remember when you asked Caroline why she was separated from Rusty? She told us that committing suicide and killing her child meant that she was stuck in her death state forever. She wasn't able to see Rusty because she was being punished for how she ended her life. If that's true, why did Barbara get a second chance? She killed a man, and she killed herself."

All the heat left my body as I processed that. Ash was right. She didn't deserve a second chance. She found a loophole and decided to wait for someone vulnerable enough to help her finish whatever she had planned.

"What am I supposed to do? Terry is never going to believe that she is anything but genuine. I don't think it's the Barbara part that she wants to vouch for. She wants it to work out with this guy so badly."

Ash sighed. "I don't know. For now, just keep an eye on her. Maybe distract yourself. Terry is going to reach her breaking point and ask for help. Until then, I don't know if anything we do will change her mind."

*

"What else is on your list?" Holden's mother, Lynn, asked me.

I was nervous about spending alone time with her, she had more than a few reasons to want me far away from her son. However, after having so much fun the other night, I finally agreed to go shopping with her.

I looked down at the print out in front of me.

"I am not even sure. Holden registered for all of this. He told me he didn't even remember getting that price gun. He just blacked out and an hour later had picked out half of the store."

She laughed. "That sounds like Holden. He loves a new project, and until the baby is here, the nursery and such feels like something he can build."

I grinned at her. He really was such a nester. Over the last couple of months, he had been bingeing on HGTV. His version of picking out a crib was dreaming about building the perfect baby room from the studs. We had plans for a nursery at home and at his parents' house for nights that we needed a date night. Lynn and Matthew had been more than excited to clean out their guest bedroom for their grandchild.

"Has he always been that way?"

"No, not always." She pushed her purse farther up on her shoulder and her eyebrows furrowed.

"No?"

"When his dad got sick, Holden felt a lot of responsibility towards him. He was always a sweet kid. He bought the most thoughtful Mother's Day presents and was always willing to help out with chores. But Matthew getting cancer rocked his world. I think it was the first time he understood that his dad wasn't invincible. He gave up college and kept the store running. I think it makes him proud, but it really broke his dad's heart at first."

"Because he gave up school?"

She nodded. "Without a second thought, he just rearranged his entire life. Holden loves it, he loves the idea of owning a business just as much as Matthew. But his dad thought he was cheating himself out of a lot of opportunities."

I blushed a little bit and moved up the aisle. If he felt that way about him not going to college, what did he think of us starting a family this young? We weren't married, we had been dating less than six months. If Holden felt obligated to be at the school before, he was never going to leave if he had a child to support. Had I ruined his life even further?

"Holden told you what's going on with his dad?" Lynn asked me.

I turned to her, gently touching her shoulder. "He did. I am so sorry. I don't know what to say."

She moved her purse to her other shoulder and seemed tired. "Nothing to say right now. But I wanted you to know that he finally understands Holden, all of him. He is looking forward to being a grandpa. It's a bright spot on his worst days. Something to look forward to."

I understood what she was offering me and gave her a grateful smile. She pulled me into a hug and then we got started on Holden's list.

*

"Are you sure this is what you want?" Holden asked, delivering me a butterscotch milkshake and a can of olives.

I grimaced at the combination even as my stomach rumbled in agreement. "Yes. But you didn't have to get that. You should be home, resting."

Holden settled onto a kitchen chair. "It's a broken wrist, babe. It's not the end of the world, and the cast will be off soon."

I shrugged. "Still, it's my fault it happened. Why are you still doing favors for me?"

"I thought that's what baby daddies did? Change diapers and buy milkshakes. There are no diapers for me right now, that leaves milkshake duty."

I knew he was joking, but I hated him calling himself baby daddy.

"You are more than that, more than just my milkshake man."

He laughed. "I know, Claire. You know, if I moved in, I would be able to rest and watch over you."

More than anything, I wanted him here with me. I wanted to have him hold my growing belly while we slept and be able to take his hand and place it over where our child rolled when I ate tomato soup. I wanted to fill out the baby book with him and lazily discuss baby names over dinner.

But "home" was a crazy place now that even I rarely felt safe in. I would suggest moving into his home with his parents if his dad wasn't recovering from chemo treatments. I had even picked up multiple apartment applications the day before to see what our options were.

"Hold, I love you. You know I do. But the whole point of you not being here all the time is so that I can watch over you. What if these shadow figures really are after you?" I asked, my arms prickling.

"Then we figure it out together."

I sighed. "Holden, please."

He sighed. "Fine, but then can we spend some time together away from here? Let's go out this weekend. To a movie, to Denny's?"

I nodded, my body relaxing as I thought of a date night. "Deal."

*

A noise on the porch brought me to the window just as I was locking the front door for the next.

"What is that?" I asked Terry, looking over at the porch.

I saw her shudder and a vision of a mutilated cat flew through my mind. Vomit climbed my throat.

"Yeah, I hope that was just a nightmare of yours and not something you really found in our yard," I told her.

She looked at me, realized I was picking up on her projections again and slowly shook her head.

"A present from Lucas last year."

I shuddered as well; it made my lower back hurt. I watched Terry slowly cross the living room and peek out of the window by the front door. She grabbed the doorknob quickly and flung the door open.

"It's Macy," she told me.

I stood up and looked over her shoulder. Macy was sitting on the porch half hidden in the dark, her makeup was a mess and tears tracked down her cheeks.

"Mac," Terry said, sitting next to her.

I followed her out and tried to squat down before realizing that if I got down, I might never get up again. I settled for putting my fingertips on Macy's shoulder. Fear filled my chest as I imagined all the things that might have gone wrong at the dance. Maybe Simon had shown up and tried something. Maybe he finished what he began outside of the gym.

"Is it Simon?" Terry asked, her fears mingling with mine and seeming to become solid in the night air.

Macy nodded. "Yes… and no. He came, and he confronted me. He found out that Shayla and I told. They called his parents and got him a lawyer. He tried touching me again. Right in front of everyone, like he was going to dance with me but was really putting his hand up my dress."

Terry reached back and gripped my arm tightly. I welcomed the pain; it kept me centered through my anger.

"Shayla screamed, and Britney came over. She punched Simon but then thought that we were upset because I had come with him. She thought I was hooking up with him and was mad. She pushed me and left with Ray. She is never going to believe that this wasn't my fault."

Terry stood suddenly. "Get in the car."

"What?" Macy said, looking terrified.

"Get in the car. He's at that Conoco by the school. He's bragging to his friends," Terry said, her face blank and unfocused.

I had no idea how she knew that but didn't doubt her for a second. Macy and I followed her to the car, and she drove us to the gas station with that same blank look. We pulled up the Conoco, the same one I took the pregnancy test in. She jumped out as soon as the car was turned off. Macy and I trailed after her. Simon was sitting on the hood of a blue car with two other boys. He looked at Terry with skepticism until Macy came into view. The look of humor he threw at her made my blood boil.

He wasn't afraid at all. He really felt like he was able to do whatever he wanted to whoever he wanted.

"Really? Is your big sister going to 'beat me up'?" Simon said, his voice condescending.

His friends laughed, but they were looking at Terry with what might have been fear.

"Terry, let's just go," Macy said, looking like a zombie with her muddled make up in the security lights.

Terry's focus finally cleared, and she looked at Simon. She leaned forward quickly and gripped his arm. He flailed it in a windmill motion, but she stayed clamped on.

"I don't need to hurt you. Shayla and Macy aren't the only ones who are going to come after you," Terry said, wearing a grin that didn't look like it belonged to her.

Macy gasped and grabbed my hand. I was able to see what Terry was seeing, images superimposed on the picture of her holding onto Simons' arm in the parking lot. Other girls, other dates that had ended in the same throes of pain and violence.

Not just forced oral sex, he had raped at least two other freshman girls who were terrified to come forward. There was so much pain and terror that belonged to this 17-year-old.

Even though he knew it wasn't possible, he knew that Terry saw all of these things. She didn't just see them; she knew the dates and was given the names like a hard candy passed to her during a kiss. Simon slowly deflated and looked at her with horror.

"And when they all know, you are going to have some very new friends that will come after you," Terry said, cocking her head.

I let go as another vision formed to take its place, one Terry was passing to Simon. Simon's mouth dropped open, and his face became ashen.

"Leave my sister alone. Don't ever touch her again," Terry whispered.

She gently dropped his arm and left him there with an unfocused expression, still swimming with visions.

Macy and I followed Terry back to the car and left Simon there in shock. I didn't know what had just happened and I didn't know if Simon would ever be held accountable for, he did. But I did know without a doubt that he would never hurt Macy again. Maybe that was enough.

Terry

Macy might be 17, but she still cleaned like she was an 11-year-old. I hated cleaning. Mom and I had a chore chart to keep on top of things, but it was more like a Bingo card. Trading duties, making bets to push the dishes off on each other or winning rock paper scissors so you didn't have to do that weekends laundry. But with Claire pregnant and working from home, it really did fall to me this time.

Sometimes I wondered if Macy played dumb so that she didn't have to help out as much. I had a feeling that was closer to the truth but also liked the idea of letting her be a kid as long as possible. I sighed and picked up the fourth crusty pair of socks off of the bathroom floor that she left for me. Well, I mostly liked the idea of her being a kid still.

When I bent over to grab a towel, I heard scuttling from behind me. I fell to my knees and whipped my head around to see behind me. Tan fingers gripped the bathroom doorway from outside. Goosebumps broke out across my body, but I was filled with excitement at the same time.

"Barbara?" I whispered.

The fingers disappeared, but the room grew cooler. I felt breath on my shoulders and turned slowly, facing the mirror. I was seeing double then I realized she was standing close to me, matching my movement exactly. I wondered how long

214

she had been following me like this, attaching to me piece by piece. Suddenly her head cocked sideways and she looked at me strangely. It looked like a smile but didn't feel like one. Something about how the grin stretched across her cheeks felt wrong and fake.

I watched her hand fall on my shoulder, and her nails dug into my skin and left a thin scratch behind. I wanted to push her away, but I was frozen. I wondered if this was a dream, but the pain was too precise to be anything but real.

In horror, I watched her raise her hand back to her face. Her nails were red with my blood. She licked them slowly. My mouth fell open slightly, and she turned me to look at her. I felt like I was moving on a turntable.

Her nails were back on my shoulder, digging into my skin. Her lips stretched until I saw her teeth lining the inside of lips. Teeth so inhuman from years of dancing with shadows. She leaned forward and bit my lower lip. Instead of feeling like a kiss, panic filled my chest.

With one movement she tugged, and a dull feeling of wetness on my chin registered in my mind. She had ripped my lip off. Barbara held it between her fingers and placed it on her tongue before swallowing it whole. Then she positioned her nails on the side of my head and forced my bleeding mouth open.

As the hole of my mouth gaped inhumanly, she pushed her fingers inside, ripping the corners of my lips. My jaw creaked with exertion then broke with a crack.

My legs gave, but Barbara stayed standing, forcing my mouth open from above. In horror I watched her shove her arm down my throat when she had a vantage point. She clawed at my neck from the inside, lapping at the blood that spurted back to her. I was paralyzed, and she was going to consume me from the inside out.

"What are you doing on the floor? Did you faint?" I heard from behind me.

I gasped and turned to see Claire standing in the doorway.

I screamed and looked around the bathroom. There was no blood, just clothes from the overturned laundry basket. I bolted to my feet and stared at myself in the mirror. The same thin lips, the same freckles, and the same intact jaw. No tearing, no bloody spit, nothing. I took a deep breath, and Claire gently touched my back, settling me.

"What happened?" she asked, looking into the mirror behind me, just like Barbara had.

"I... thought I saw a spider in the laundry basket. When I fell, I thought it might have gotten on me."

She laughed, obviously relieved.

"Do you want me to help you look? I will kill it for you."

I shook my head. "I think I am going to take a shower after I get these clothes in the washer."

"Okay," Claire squeezed my shoulder and headed back to her room to write.

I sank to the ground and began picking up the clothes, crying quietly and looking over my shoulder for Barbara. Had it really come to this? I wanted to know her to have a chance to remember Kerry. But was I supposed to be part of this? Or did she just want me out of the way? Could I exist while she lived out the life, she thought she deserved?

More than anything I didn't want that to be true. I wanted for us to become one, but I was beginning to wonder if attempting to live in the past was going to annihilate me. Maybe it wasn't the escape I desperately needed it to be. Maybe I would be violently erased altogether.

*

I wanted to be able to look through these photo albums and be comforted by the memories they held, but I wasn't. Every day captured here filled me with anger for all the moments that we had lost, not realizing how precious they were while they were happening. The amount of regret I held in my heart made me sick.

I held a snapshot of my mom on Halloween, dressed as a gypsy with her best friend Missy and doubled over laughing.

As my fingers touched the edge, I felt another photo underneath. I carefully pulled it out and gasped. It was a photo of Barbara, her curly brown hair catching the sunlight. She was holding onto the necklace that Kerry had given her. Maybe this was a celebration photo. One she was able to look back on as the beginning of their life together, the promise he actually kept.

I wondered how it got into our photo album and slid it out. The photo landed carefully in my lap and a suggestion clouded over my vision, bringing me into it.

"Hey, I know we aren't really talking right now. But I wanted to return these. I know much you love them," CJ said after letting himself into the back door.

I was sitting at the kitchen table reading. He placed my Princess Bride and High school musical DVD's on the table. During our last real movie night, we had watched them, a massive bowl of popcorn between us and kissing between scenes. My heart hurt to remember that, it felt so long ago.

"Thank you," I said, motioning for him to sit.

He looked grateful, and we fell into conversation like we always had. There was this moment, it seemed like a small moment, but it was like destiny opening up to me and giving me a chance to really make a choice. CJ belonged to the Terry in this life. I was surer of it than I had ever been sure of anything else. It was possible to kiss him now and tie our souls together for the rest of our life. It would be easy.

I stood up and made my way to the cast-iron skillet setting on the stove to dry. We had used it to make dinner last night, and I had wiped it out this morning. I saw my fingers wrap around the handle and carried it across the kitchen to where CJ was sitting. Without any reservation, I swung the pan, and it connected with the back of his head. He fell to the ground, looking up at me in hurt confusion.

I knew that it wasn't me doing it, but there was hardly any distinction between Barbara and me anymore. She knew that he belonged to me and for her to finally have her future with Kerry, CJ couldn't be a part of my life. Barbara was willing to take any lengths necessary to make sure he wouldn't get in the way.

"Ter?" he said, his voice garbled.

I straddled him and brought the pan high over my head. "Terry doesn't live here anymore."

As the skillet connected with his forehead, I heard a wet cracking noise.

I screamed as I fell back into myself. The photo in my lap was gone, if it had ever really been there at all. My arms and legs shook like they contained static. I had always felt like CJ might be hurt if we were together, but I had never suspected that it would be because I was somehow capable of hurting him. But it was too late now. My soul was intertwined with Barbara's, and there was a darkness in her that would not be satisfied until Kerry was back in our arms. CJ didn't have a place in my life, even as a friend. He wasn't safe as long as Barbara was attached to my soul.

Leaving him was kinder.

Chapter 10

Claire

"Do you have any predictions?" I asked Holden, rubbing my hands over my belly.

I had gained more weight in the last three months than felt possible. It didn't feel humanly possible to be this hungry all of the time. Holden was endlessly amused by the way my belly button stuck out now.

He took a deep breath and leaned back in his hard-plastic chair. We were alone in a darkened room waiting for our ultrasound technician.

"You're the psychic one," Holden said, smiling at me.

I rolled my eyes. "Come on. You've refused to say anything either way."

He leaned forward and kissed my cheek. "What's the point? As long as the baby is healthy, it doesn't matter if it's a boy or a girl."

"Terry and Macy think it's a huge deal. They have been on one team or another for the past month. I think they have money on it."

He chuckled. "What about you?"

I closed my eyes. My sisters had asked me over and over, but I acted like I didn't have an idea one way or another. I didn't want to ruin the surprise. I had sensed this baby's presence since before I really knew I was pregnant.

"It's a boy."

He lit up and rubbed his palms together subconsciously. "Really?"

I grinned at him. "Yes. Does that make you happy?"

Holden kissed my belly with gentleness. "So happy. Now I won't be quite as outnumbered in that house."

I laughed. "It's not that bad."

The technician let herself in and rubbed lubricant on my belly.

"Ready?" she asked.

"It's a boy, I just have this feeling," Holden said with an air of authority.

I giggled.

The technician indulged him and rubbed the stick over my abdomen.

"Well, I guess Dad has some pretty great intuition. Look here, it's a boy. Congratulations."

I looked at the curve of his spine on the high-resolution screen. I saw his button nose and his thumb disappear into his mouth. He was beautiful, so beautiful.

Holden gripped my arm, and I felt a rush of emotion from him. He stared at the screen and would have seemed terrified if not for the goofy grin. It was hard to love him this much, it made the stakes much higher.

I caught snapshots of wishes and dreams. He hoped our baby boy would have my green eyes and his tanned skin. He dreamed of him finding comfort in his arms and wanted to count every single yawn. I saw them playing baseball in our backyard. I saw him look down to see a simple ring on his fourth finger, his arm around me at the movies fifty years down the road. I nodded without realizing it, agreeing to every single one of these future memories. Wanting them more than anything else in the world.

*

"Mom, we are supposed to be focusing," I said, laughing as I caught her staring at my belly once again.

She shook her head, grinning. "I just can't get used to it. When I am… wherever I am, I am not able to keep an eye on you guys. It's part of the arrangement. I just see you as an eighteen-year-old, barely graduating high school and still dating Ken. It's hard to imagine you and Holden starting a family together."

I cocked my head. "Did you ever see us ending up together?"

My mom gave my hand a squeeze. "I tried not to look because you hated it. But yes, that was one thing about you that has been set in stone since the two of you met. I saw the way he looked at you in the future, the way he already did. But you had to find your way to looking back at him in your own time.

Even though I saw your children and your wedding, I never really thought it was something that was real. Like, it was too beautiful to be true."

"Wedding?!" I asked in a panic, staring at her.

She pressed her lips together. "Where were we?"

It was clear she thought she said too much and went back to meditating. A wedding and children, more than one? Even moving in together scared me, but I had to admit that hearing my mom's vision of what our future might be made me hopeful. More than that, it was something I realized that I wanted. I wanted Holden, the simple rings and kids playing in the yard. But the more I wanted it, the more afraid I was of losing it.

Sighing, I closed my eyes and focused on building up my wall. The threat of Barbara did make the stakes higher, and my focus narrower. The more time I spent in this half-world, the clearer I saw the shadow figures.

In this world, my mom created a wall of light around us that was impenetrable, giving me time to work. But it was temporary. Sooner or later my wall would be all I had, giving me no other option but to make it a fortress.

My mom might be part of another reality now, but I saw that the shadow figures scared her as well. She shuddered when their iris-less voids bored into her. I saw her need to rub the goosebumps from her arms. After about an hour of spackling the bricks and meditating, I was exhausted and opened my eyes. We both fell back, tired from the exertion.

"Mom, can you see what's going on right now at home? With Barbara and…. Len."

I saw from the way that she hugged her self that the pain had reached her regardless of how far away she was right now.

"Do you blame me?" she asked, her face contorting.

I recognized her demeanor from a million arguments while I was growing up. When I screamed at her and told her she was the reason anything went wrong in my life. Those memories made me sick, and I wished for the chance to start over for the millionth time. I couldn't start over, but I was able to give her peace.

"No, Mom. Of course not. I just wonder what I was like back then. Did you suspect anything? Did Dad?" I asked.

My mom shook her head. "Nothing like this. I once heard you telling Ash about a boy you met at the lake. You had just had your first kiss and were so excited. I didn't want to take any happiness away from you by pushing you to share it with me."

"Yeah, I remember that too. I was excited to have an older boy interested in me. That was before things changed. In the beginning, he just paid attention to me, and I needed it at that moment in my life. I guess even then he was trying to get me ready for what he had planned. I was young."

She pulled me closer to her. "Exactly. You were young. What he did, what men like this do, groom you so slowly that what happens afterward feels like your choice. But it wasn't. He preyed on you. He knew better. And you did the only thing you could."

"What?"

"You got through it. You recognized it for what it was and have decided to take control back."

I smiled, feeling hopeful for the first time in months.

"Why can't you be my spiritual guide?" I asked, not wanting her to leave already.

My mom had admitted that she didn't send Barbara, but that didn't mean as much as I thought it did. My mom sent messages of a kind but wasn't in charge of who I ended up with. She was just a spirit; she had no power over the universe. However, she did agree that Barbara wasn't who I was meant to be guided by and she might be keeping my real guide from me.

My mom gave me a sad smile. "Because I don't have any unfinished business. I loved you girls with my entire heart, it was all I wanted in the world. Being a spirit guide is two-pronged. They are here to help you, but they are also there to earn their way into oblivion."

I nodded, already having a feeling but wanting her regardless.

"I just... it's not just me that needs help. Were you able to see Terry's future because she was more open to it? How her future collides with Barbara's? She is throwing away her life with CJ and is all caught up in this complete stranger. She's... different. It's hard not to be afraid for her sometimes."

"Afraid for her or *of* her?"

I blushed. "Both."

My mom sighed. "I never saw this. I can't tell you what I saw because it's still on course as far as I am concerned, but I have a feeling this wasn't part of her original path. I think you should contact a past life counselor for her."

I grabbed a pad of paper off of the coffee table. "A past life counselor? What do they do?"

She laughed. "Counsel her old soul? I am not quite sure. Missy knows more about it than me. But I have a feeling they will be able to find out exactly what happened to Barbara, then we will know what her spirit needs to move on."

"I don't think she wants that. She is lost in this life."

"Exactly. She is lost, she might need some rescuing."

*

"This feels pretty familiar," Macy said, grinning at Holden as he passed her the dish of chicken parmesan.

I smiled back at them. Holden had seemed to come into my life right when I needed him. I had just lost my mother and was thrust into being Macy's guardian. I was completely unsure of myself and heading into a self-destructive cycle. Then I ran into Holden at the grocery store where he worked, and he brought us dinner. He changed my life and gave me the strength to believe in myself again.

"Familiar bad?" Holden asked, taking a massive bite of chicken.

"Not at all. It's just what I was craving," I told them.

Macy gave me a disgusted look, making me laugh.

"I'm talking about the pasta," I told her, pointing my fork at her.

Knowing he was here to help me, especially when Terry's priorities were so skewered, really meant a lot to me. I might not have been sure about where Holden and I were going to end up, but I never doubted that we were a team. When he found out what happened to Macy, we had to stop him from going to Simon himself. I had never seen that side of him and was touched by his ferocity when protecting his family, including my sisters. I would never have to stand alone again.

Terry

February 2016

I want to feel happy as I watch my sisters swing in the hammock together outside. For my whole life, I just wanted things to be easy between us, and I had promised to work harder to accept Claire into our lives. But seeing them wrapped in a comforter out there, talking and laughing, all I can think of is how it's so easy for them to find love in their lives. I didn't understand why life was easy for them when I was the one who seemed to try the hardest.

I was the one who tried to keep us together, who made birthday cakes and kept special events on the calendar. I was the one who came to school plays, who kept track of friendships so that my conversations with them mattered. I was the one who encouraged them to do well in school and watched over them. I don't think they had ever once said thank you.

Macy just floated through life, getting into trouble with boys and cheating on Britney. She barely tried with her grades and spent more time at cheer practice than filling out college applications. Regardless, college would be much easier for her than it was for me. And Claire, she had it all. She graduated and was okay with being away from home. But after the accident, she became the hero. She was there for Macy, weaseling her way into her heart and becoming her protector. She was able to fall in love with Holden and start a family. Did she really deserve it all?

What did I have? A job I was afraid of? A college degree I didn't get to use but was drowning in debt because of? A best friend that refused to talk to me? A man I was cosmically tied to, but who was kissing another girl goodnight? What did it take to tip the scales so that I was able to have it all instead?

Maybe it wasn't impossible. Maybe it was as easy as just allowing myself to slip in Barbara.

I gripped the box of matches I was holding. I was planning on lighting some scented candles and soaking in the bath to relax. But... what if I took the matches outside instead?

What if I lit one and touched it to the comforter that grazed the porch as the girls swung in the light wind. What if I spun the hammock and tangled them up in the burning blanket? What if I stood and watched them scream so that I was able to consume the life they left behind?

"Ter? What's with the matches?" Macy asked.

My feet froze, and I realized with a shock that I had walked outside. I was standing in front of the hammock still gripping the book of matches. I dropped them, Claire and Macy looking at me with worry. I recalled the vision of them strangling in fire and was revolted. In the back of my mind, I heard Barbara giggle.

"I was cleaning the kitchen and must have grabbed them on autopilot," I lied, knowing I was doing a lousy job of it.

Claire opened the blanket and smiled at me, throwing me a life preserver.

"There's room for one more. You must be freezing."

I climbed in carefully, making sure I didn't squish my nephew. I took a breath of their mingled perfumes and buried my head in Claire's shoulder. I shook, but it wasn't all from the still frozen backyard.

*

I had been on Eli's Facebook page so much in the last couple of months that my account had taken to updating me whenever he posted anything new. Usually, it felt like a little present throughout the day, like he was telling me he was thinking of me. But today, today it was a post he was tagged in. A photograph of him and Kristy with a countdown to their wedding. His profile didn't even say that they were engaged.

The last time we talked he told me he was drawn to me and wanted to come visit. Why would he say that if he and Kristy were serious? As if reading my mind, his name popped up on my instant messenger.

Hey, good morning

Morning

How is your day going?

Fine

Okay, Terry. What's wrong? Did I catch you at a bad time?

I took a screenshot of the update and sent it to him. I watched his message bubble blink as he wrote back.

I'm sorry you had to see that. I had no idea how to tell you.

How long have you been engaged?

About a year. Before I knew you were out there.

I don't understand. Why are we talking if you are getting married? What about you coming here?

I bit my lip, drawing blood. I didn't want this to be the end of our chapter before I even got a chance to try.

It doesn't change anything, in fact, it makes it even more important. Did you have someone else in your life before you woke up and had your new memories?

I blushed, looking at the photo of CJ and me on my desk. Before friending Eli, I had discreetly deleted a lot of pictures off of my profile. CJ barely went online and didn't even notice, but I still felt like I was hiding a husband in my attic.

Not like that, I was never engaged to him. And now, we aren't together at all because he knows how I feel about you.

It's more complicated for me. I thought I loved Kristy. But it's like you getting your memories back sent out a beacon to mine. I just woke up one day and looked at Kristy differently. My heart didn't belong to just her anymore. She would never understand, and a five-year relationship can't just be ended overnight.

What are we going to do?

I have to come see you, before the wedding. I have to know if this is real.

My stomach shook with excitement and I closed down the messenger. The feeling of déjà vu was heavy in my chest. This was beginning to feel just like Kerry and Barbara's situation. Eli was coming to me, which I loved. But it was in secret. He still cared about his fiancé enough to have to hide his tracks.

What is going to happen when he is here? Would we make love? Did he plan on making me promises? Kerry had made Barbara the same assurances before and ended up leaving regardless. Were we bound to repeat the same mistakes they did?

I wondered if it was something I should have ever started in the first place. Kerry left a hole so big in Barbara that she needed more than one life to fix it. I didn't think I had the strength to live through that kind of heartbreak a second time.

Chapter 11

Sleeping was usually my escape. My ridiculous pregnancy dreams were something that I looked forward to telling Holden about the next morning. They were hilarious, until a couple of weeks ago. They were becoming dark and terrifying. I was waking up stiff with fear and unable to move. I hadn't felt like this since I first started seeing the shadow figures.

It began with my dream changing in little ways that left me feeling weary but unsure of what was wrong. The people in my dreams seemed more like very lifelike dolls rather than my loved ones. A slightly different chin, a nose that was just a little bit off. Black masses whipped in and out of my peripheral vision.

I laid in bed with my limbs full of concrete, my sight wandering around my room and seeking out masses in the corner that were waiting to crawl into bed with me. Holden staying over more often helped a little, but the dreams were coming back with a vengeance.

Tonight, seemed no different. I woke up, the dream still lingering in my mind and crystallizing my skin again. I panted, my fingers tingling back to life. I took a deep breath and smiled over at Holden, who was deep in sleep with his mouth open and one arm draped across his pillow. I gently brushed his hair out his face and leaned forward to kiss his cheek. As I sat up, I saw a body like blackout across the room. Shoulders with no real shape, bottomless red voids set into their faces, and breathing that sounded like it was coming through mottled cotton.

I tried to look away, but the eyes trapped mine, as they always did. They weren't satisfied with catching me meditating and having to scale my wall anymore. They found me half asleep, whispering to me and holding me like I was in a trance. The shadow solidified, stepping away from the wall using the power that it was drawing from me. It pulled me to him, pleading and sick.

I slid from the bed, trying to pull back while it opened its arms and called me to him. Begging me to open myself up to him. I tried to look away, I tried to cut off the connection and wondered if they were able to lead me to the shadowland while I was still awake. The shadow became more explicit and I saw the fuzzy brown hair of Barbara. But something was different now.

I wasn't seeing the Barbara she had tried to show me in the beginning, I saw the real Barbara in her death form. The waterlogged version of Caroline flashed in my mind, and I shuddered violently. Barbara gave me a crooked grin and knew I saw her as she truly was. She gave me it all.

Her clothes were soaked with blood, dotting her shoulders heavily. Barbara shrugged, the low light in the room just enough to reflect off the gun she was holding. A weapon that couldn't hurt me anymore, it had already done its job. Barbara slowly opened her mouth, and I was able to see the wall behind her. It took me a moment to realize I was able to see the wall from inside of that gaping broken hole. She reached out and snatched up my hand. She wasn't talking, but I heard her voice inside of my head.

"I can't make you get rid of the baby. But I can make you like me; I can make dying what you want more than anything."

My fingers got close to her mouth. It really wasn't a mouth anymore, just a jagged opening. Her gums hung in strips and her bone fractured into points. I knew she was right, if my hand went all the way through and plunged into whatever remained of her haunted mind, I would lose mine completely. This would give her permission to enter me whenever she wanted. She would be able to make me hurt my baby, and I would be powerless to stop her.

I was able to cry but I wasn't able to move in any other way, I felt like I was operating on an assembly line. The smell of metallic blood and the last voids of her life filled my nostrils.

"Claire!" Holden sat up, horrified and scared.

I screamed, leaning to pull myself away. I inched my head over the tiniest amount and saw the dirty hands covering my

236

own, moving me like a puppet. Holden jolted to his feet and gathered me into his arms. As soon as I lost eye contact with Barbara, I was freed and collapsed. Nausea overcame me. I heaved violently and held onto my belly, terrified.

"What was that?" he yelled, holding me so tightly he was hurting my back.

"Barbara, she was trying… she was trying…" I stuttered, shivering.

He pulled back to look at me. "To do what? To hurt the baby? To make you, do it?"

I nodded, feeling sick and clammy.

Holden tried to stand up while still holding onto me. "What do I do? I don't know how to help. Can't you just turn it off?"

As scared as I was, this was still able to make me see red. This wasn't a choice that I was making. What kind of mother did he think I was?

"Turn what off? Seeing ghosts?"

"Yes! Claire, if you have this connection, you are risking our baby's life."

I stopped shivering, warming up with anger. "This isn't my fault. I didn't choose this."

"Are you stopping it either?"

"How?"

"Give it up. Find some way to give up this gift, or you are not going to be able to save our child. What means more to you?" Holden asked, his face red.

I pushed him away. "Are you joking me? This *gift* was what my mom wanted most for me. It helps people. How dare you twist it into something bad? It's not the gift, its Barbara."

"Who you keep allowing into our home over and over."

"Our home?" I stood up, still shaky.

This is the thing I was most afraid of, Holden seeing my gift as something that brought heartbreak to my family. Something that made me different, someone irresponsible and untrustworthy. He promised he would never become my dad, but this didn't feel like love and support.

"Get out. This is *my* home."

He flushed, and his mouth was set into a tight line. "Are you joking? Who is going to protect you when that psycho comes back?"

"I will. I don't need you making me feel like a bad parent or some kind of basket case. I am new at this, but it's not a mistake. Leave."

"Claire."

"Now," I yelled.

I heard Macy's door shut as she came to see what was going on.

"Are you okay?" she asked, her hair crazy with sleep.

Holden glared at me. "Fine. I'll leave."

She looked at me, confused and worried.

"Good," I said, crying.

"Watch her, okay? She isn't thinking clearly. Barbara attacked her again."

As Holden stormed out, Macy took his place and sat next to me on the bed.

"What happened?" she asked, wrapping her arms around me.

"Barbara came back. She was trying to make me hurt the baby," I forced out, holding my belly protectively.

"Are you okay?" Macy asked, leaning back to look me over.

"Yes!" I said, tired of people asking me all the time.

She gripped me closer. "Stop. We care, that's why we are asking."

"But Holden…"

Macy shook her head. "No, Holden isn't wrong. He didn't grow up with this. He has no idea how scary and precious these gifts are. All he knows is that something is happening, something that might hurt his child. He has no way of helping you. Can you imagine?"

I wanted to argue with her, but there was no point. I saw the ghosts and still couldn't do anything to protect myself. I had no idea what it was like to sit on the edge and wonder. But seeing the fear up close and personal didn't make it any easier to digest.

"It just makes me feel like a terrible mom already. Like this is my fault, that I asked to be hurt because of my gift. Like… maybe Holden will reach his breaking point and leave me."

"Like Dad left Mom," Macy said.

I nodded.

"Never. Never, Claire. It's not the same thing. He is scared because he loves you. He didn't run away, you asked him to leave."

Maybe Holden wasn't like my dad, but that didn't mean he understood what this gift meant to me. It didn't mean that it wouldn't come between us. Would I let him down? Was I able to love him and my child enough to find the balance that my parents couldn't?

*

"I don't know if this will work. I feel stupid," Terry said, crossing her legs and looking like the idea of past life counseling was equal to using a Ouija board.

"You don't have to do anything, you just have to relax," Missy said.

Missy had not only known a lot more about past life counseling, she thought that she would be able to do the session herself. After the betrayal of Barbara, we were leery to trust someone entirely new. This made Missy the perfect person for the job.

Also, Terry needed extra convincing that Barbara was terrible all the way through. Her attacking me didn't seem to be enough so far.

We all held hands and allowed our energy to flow between each other, making us stronger. It was crazy how much their power felt like who they were as a person. Macy was super light and bouncy, dancing through my arms. Terrys was constant and solid. Missy was sure and wispy, like champagne at the back of my throat. I wondered what mine felt like.

"Okay, Terry. I need you to close your eyes and concentrate on your toes. They are warm and relaxed. Let them go, relax into the warmth. Let that feeling travel up your body until it's all that you are aware of."

Terry cracked on eye open. "Seriously?"

"Sleep," Missy said, her voice sounding like it was melding with a thousand others, loud even though it was a whisper.

Terry slumped, and I laughed in shock.

"How do we talk to her if she is asleep?" Macy asked, clapping in front of Terry's face.

"It's not her we want to talk to," Missy said, concentrating.

The air in the room whipped around us, calling to Barbara. A thin scream pierced the air. Terry slowly sat up and opened her eyes. Macy gasped when she realized that Terry's eyes had changed from green to brown. My arm broke out in painful goosebumps, and I wanted to rip my hand from hers.

"Hold on girls, I need your help to keep her here. She's not going to want to talk to me," Missy said, gripping my fingers.

I nodded, not able to look away from Barbara hiding inside of Terry. A snarl stretched across my sister's mouth, over Barbara's.

"Well, this is a fun trick. Do I get to wear her forever or am I just visiting?" she sneered.

"Visiting. I just wanted to find out why you are attached to Terry. I am not completely convinced you used to belong to her. I think that you preyed on her because she came back from her coma so sad, her body weak and destroyed. I think you want her to finish whatever it is that you left undone."

Terry twitched, and it was clear that it was painful for Terry to let Barbara hold onto her like this. Barbara shook her head, her teeth clenched tightly.

"Yes, you will tell me," Missy said firmly.

A laugh bubbled out of Terry's throat, giving me chills.

"I know that he left you. I know that his wife was pregnant," I said, surprised by the venom in my voice.

"Ex-wife," Barbara hissed, squeezing my fingers until they were white.

"It didn't matter. He left you, for her. He wanted a family more than he wanted you."

She was crying. It was clear that it was an emotion that stemmed from rage, not sadness.

242

"That's right, bitch. I was supposed to start a family with him. She probably sabotaged her birth control, and he went back. But it didn't last. I paid them a visit, a visit to last a lifetime."

"A visit to last a lifetime or end a life?" Missy asked.

I fought the urge to cover my ears, not wanting to hear the answer.

Barbara laughed. "I ended one life, but not the life I wanted to end. He wasn't who I wanted to suffer."

"Just one?" Missy asked, leaning forward to pluck at Terry's shirt.

Barbara's spirit was layered on top of hers, and we saw flashes of her blood-soaked outfit.

"Two, if we are being technical. But do I really count?"

"What now? You killed Kerry. What do you want now? Why are you reconnecting with him? Why are you trying to hurt Claire?" Macy asked.

Barbara shook her head. "I don't give a fuck about Claire. I want to hurt that delicious little soul inside of her. I missed my chance to rid the world of unwanted, inconvenient pregnancies once. I will not miss that chance again."

I pulled myself away and stood up. Macy pulled back and came up behind me, holding me protectively.

Missy let go of Barbara's hand, and we felt the connection break with a snap. Barbara had arrived with a scream but left without a whisper. Terry slumped before her head snapped back up, her eyes green again.

"Did you hear all of that?" Macy asked.

She nodded. "I am so sorry. But... I would never let her hurt you or the baby."

"Do you even have a choice?" I asked her, turning away and leaving before I could hear her defend Barbara.

I understood her wanting to know who Kerry's soul was now. I realized that love made you crazy. But what about her love for me? For her nephew? Did he mean more to her than us? Did his life have more meaning than mine?

*

Stumbling knocks upstairs woke me from a bad dream, and I almost fell out of bed. I looked at the alarm clock next to my head. 2:30 am. It sounded like Macy was doing Zumba in the living room again. I crept upstairs and saw that the light in my mom's room was on, shadows dancing on the walls. I gently pushed open the door.

I had expected to see my mom's bed, her desk, and her photos. Instead, I saw a beautiful cherry wood crib with decals of Winnie the Pooh dancing above it. A rocking chair and changing table piled with receiving blankets and diapers. I saw my sisters, sweaty as they moved a dresser against the wall.

"Claire!" Macy said, dropping her side of the dresser.

"What happened?" I asked, not wanting to cry.

Terry sat in front of me. "I know. Mom's stuff, we moved it into storage yesterday when you were out to dinner with Ash. We can go through it later and decide what we want to do. But this is the biggest room in the house and Macy, and I thought you might need it. It would be easy to move your bed up here if you want to share it with him for the first year or so. When he is old enough, we will convert half of it into a playroom."

I looked around, seeing the memories she drew in front of me. "You did this all for me?"

Macy sat next to her. "Of course."

"I meant what I said. I want my nephew to grow up here, this is your home. And Holden's, when you're ready. This is where he should be, with us," Terry said, hugging me.

I nodded, the tears coming anyway. But this time, because I knew I belonged. Because they surprised me with a future that was set in stone. Because they wanted me.

*

This was familiar, showing up at Holden's grocery store and hoping to win him over. Last year I had pushed him away and nearly broken up with him. He was so hurt, and I begged him to understand and take me back. Now, it was impossible to imagine my life without him, and somehow that terrified me even more. I carried a wrapped box against growing belly and smiled at Cheri, my favorite cashier.

Holden and I had talked after our argument, and he forgave me, he always did. But there was an unspoken awkwardness between us now that I hated.

"Hi! Any idea where Holden is?" I asked.

"In the back, I think he is having his last fifteen-minute break," she said, gently rubbing my belly as I walked past.

I pushed my way through the rubber double doors at the back of the store and found Holden sitting at a plastic table eating a sandwich.

"Hey, babe. This is a nice surprise," Holden said, standing up and kissing me on the cheek.

He was smiling, but the lines of his shoulders showed how weary he truly was. He wanted to move on but was still so worried and didn't want to have another huge confrontation where he was rejected. He needed something more than an apology and promise that things would be different.

"Yeah, I brought you something."

"I can see that. Can I open it now? I only have a few minutes before I have to go back."

I nodded and gave it to him. Sweat trailed down my back as he gently tore the paper off the box, revealing a new pot set.

"Thank you?" he said, laughing a little.

"I know. Kind of weird. We might need them for this new chapter in our life. And… a year ago I told you that you were my pot lid and I meant that. I want you to keep this new pot set in our kitchen," I said, blushing to my hairline.

246

Holden grinned. "Our kitchen?"

"Is that still, okay? You don't have to if you don't want to."

Holden stepped forward and pulled me into a kiss. "I said it then, and I'll say it now. You will never be a lonely pot ever again. I accept."

I let out a huge breath. A huge part of me was convinced he was going to say no. I felt weak with relief.

"I love you," I whispered.

Right on cue, our son kicked between us, making Holden laugh.

"I know, babe. I love you too."

Terry

"Thanks again for doing this," I told CJ, giving him another cardboard box to put into my trunk.

We had put a lot of my mom's belongings into storage when turning her room into the nursery, but there was a lot that just needed to go to Goodwill. Clothes she hadn't worn since the 80s, multiples of books she had read a million times, and boxes of baking equipment that she hadn't even opened. It was a big job, and I needed help lifting the heaviest of the boxes I packed. CJ was the first person I thought of, he always made things like this fun. However, I was surprised that he had even answered the phone.

But he did. He came that same afternoon and helped me without making me feel bad about it.

"No problem. What did Claire think of the new room?" he asked.

"She loved it but seemed shocked that we wanted her to stay."

CJ sat down and took a swig from his water bottle. "Can you blame her?"

"What do you mean?" I asked, bristling.

He shrugged. "Things have been weird. I can see why she would think you wouldn't want her here."

I blushed and wanted to feel angry, but he was right.

"Well, I do. That's why I am taking care of all of this. Because we are a family."

CJ stared at me. I was suddenly sorry I asked him here at all. It was hard for him to just be here for me after how hard the last couple of months had been.

We had to talk about it. We had to bring up our fight, why we had been avoiding each other. Whether or not we had a future even as friends. But right now, I was exhausted, mentally and physically.

"CJ, I know I shouldn't have asked you to help me. But when I think about someone, I would call in the middle of the night to be there for me, it's always you. It's always been you," I said, breaking eye contact with him to look at my bare feet.

I heard him sigh. "I know. That's why I came. But when I tried to be there for you the way I thought I should be, the way I thought you wanted me to be, you pushed me away. I have no idea what you want from me right now."

"What if it's just to be my friend?" I asked, terrified of what he would say.

CJ turned to look at me, and my eyes dragged their way up to his. "Is that really what you want? I know there's a part of you that belongs to this random Eli guy. But I still feel like there's part of you that is supposed to belong to me."

I watched tears make a trail down to his chin and had to keep myself from kissing them away. He was right. When he touched my skin, my skin called back to him. He was my best friend, my other half in so many ways. I pictured a crazy happy future with him easily. But it wasn't fair to do that to him when I was also calling out for whoever Eli ended up being. CJ had half of my heart, but that wasn't enough for him. And it shouldn't be. I was killing him, and it was killing me.

"I don't know," I said, unsure of how to begin.

He reached for the back of my neck, bringing his lips up to mine hesitantly. As I responded to him the way my body wanted to, it became clear that I had the power to choose right now. I could kiss him and extinguish whatever hold Barbara had over my past. Choosing CJ was possible.

As our bodies pressed together, I saw swirling gray smoke and held back a scream. Her fingers clawed the inside of my chest, my throat. I felt her climbing into me, attempting to make my decision for me before I ruined her plan. She ripped through my body savagely and slapped CJ as he leaned in.

His mouth dropped open with disbelief, and his hand flew to his cheek where redness was already blooming. She wanted to destroy him, to take the tape dispenser and cut his throat with the serrated edge. She wanted to lick the blood off of her fingers. I shivered and used all my strength to push her further down.

"Please, leave," I spat out.

CJ stood up, he was sweaty and embarrassed. He hesitated, looking back at me.

"She's doing this to you, isn't she?"

She shook my head violently. "Leave now!"

I tried to reach up and touch him, wanting to comfort him. Instead, Barbara forced screams from my throat, leaving it raw. CJ was crying but left, taking the tape dispenser with him when he saw how I was looking at it.

With him gone, I collapsed onto the floor of the nursery. I took ragged breaths. I was completely losing control. How far would she go to get what she wanted? Would she hurt Claire? Macy? What would happen if CJ came back? What would happen when she was finally reunited with Kerry? I was awake this time, locked in my body but able to see what she was doing. I felt like a zombie, a dead body being reanimated. I needed to get away from her.

I stood up, Barbara was spent from her efforts and sank back into me. I grabbed my purse and abandoned my shoes. The further I walked off into the night, the further I got from the house, the stronger I became.

I felt like running away forever. Maybe Kerry would meet me somewhere, and Barbara would get precisely what she has always wanted. Perhaps I could live in her dreams forever and keep my family safe. Maybe they were better off without me.

*

I had smashed my phone on the way to the park, but my sisters found me anyway. I sensed them before they came into view at all. I didn't look in their direction as they both sat on a swing next to me, one on each side.

"How did you find me?" I asked quietly.

"CJ called and told us you were upset. Then, I found your aura trail and followed it," Macy answered, turning in her swing to look at me.

I looked at her. "I didn't know that was possible."

"Me either. But it turns out auras get really strong when you are upset. Once I focused it wasn't really that hard. What happened? Did you guys get into another fight?" she asked.

I shook my head. "It's not just the fighting. Sometimes when I am with him, it's easy to want to just forget all of this Barbara and Eli stuff and just be with him. A part of me thinks that's the right path for me. But it's hard to ignore all of these memories and feelings. And when I am leaning towards being with him… Barbara chooses for me."

Claire stiffened next to me; fear rolled off of her in waves. Anger surged up in my stomach. Why would she be afraid of me? She wasn't having her body stolen from her. Why was she blaming me?

"She chooses for you?" Claire asked, getting off her swing to sit in the gravel in front of me.

I nodded. "Yes. She's getting stronger and can kind of override my body. It's terrifying."

"Is she here now?" Macy asked.

Claire and I shook our head at the same time.

"When I am not at home, it's easier to hide from her. I don't know if she can really leave the house. Yet," I tell them, and Macy lets out a relieved breath.

"What should we do?" Macy asks, sitting next to Claire.

"What do you want to do?" Claire asks me.

All my anger evaporated as she gave her trust over to me.

"I really don't know. I am tired all the time. I'm scared of Barbara going too far and hurting me. Or accidentally hurting someone else. I think... I need help," I tell her, sobbing and dropping to the ground in front of her.

Claire and Macy wrapped me in their arms and held me.

"Taking a break is a good idea, you need to get away and let yourself get strong while we make a plan," Macy said into my shoulder.

Claire sat back. "Exactly. Let's go somewhere, take that trip you wanted to take last summer. Let's rent that beach house. When we come back you will be refreshed and stronger. We will tackle this together."

I leaned back to look at them, sobbing but sure. I was damaged and broken, but I was still theirs. I wasn't alone. I didn't want to hurt them.

"I can't go back home," I whispered.

Claire nodded and pulled out of her cell phone.

"Ash? Hey, I need a favor."

Chapter 12

Claire

April 2016

This trip to the beach meant so much to me. It was the trip we were supposed to take last summer. When I thought about my sister and Mom visiting me after graduation and the night we watched Dirty Dancing, it was hard to breathe. It was a perfect moment, but there were so many expectations hanging in the air. When Ash texted me, I was relieved to be able to leave. I had to be difficult, I had to keep my mom trailing after me and forcing her to prove herself. To show that she cared about me.

But what if I had just gone? What if that was the trip that would have healed all that laid broken between us and changed the course of our life? Would I have been home already when I got the news of my book deal? Would I have been able to cheer Terry on when she received her service award? Would we have lingered at dinner, visiting and laughing. Would Lucas have gotten tired of waiting and just went home instead? Would my mom still be alive?

Choking back emotion, I looked at my sisters down on the beach. They were attempting to start a fire for dinner. It was impossible to go back and give them all the memories I had stolen from them, but maybe this could be a trip of a lifetime as well. The trip that saved Terry instead.

"Hey! I got it started. Bring on the wieners!" Macy yelled up to me.

Terry laughed. "It's been a long time since you have said anything like that, right?"

I snorted. Macy being gay had felt taboo for so long. But after her last fight with Dad, it was pointless to not embrace it with my whole heart. Macy hiding from herself had caused more than a few problems during her senior year.

We roasted hot dogs and ate them with mustard right from the stick. Macy challenged us to a smores cook-off and pulled out a bag stuffed to the brim with treats to use. It looked like she had been stocking up for months. Terry tried an Oreo smores which would have been delicious if she hadn't tried to talk us into eating it with a potato chip on top. It fell apart, but she looked like she loved the result. I made mine with Chip Ahoy and chocolate syrup, which would have won if Macy hadn't expanded on my idea with one Chip Ahoy, one Oreo, and topped the melted marshmallow with a square of cookies and cream bar. After our unconventional dinner, the long drive caught up with us, and we went up to bed.

I was convinced I wasn't going to be able to sleep in the unfamiliar bed, and my back ached in pulses. But I passed out immediately.

A creaking noise woke me hours later. I saw a crib in the corner of the room. I saw my son roll and carefully tuck his small thumb into his rosebud mouth.

I didn't question why he was here and not in my belly. I didn't wonder where the crib came from and why it was at the beach. But when I saw the dark mass standing at the foot of the crib, I was filled with terror and confusion.

The body looked like Terry, but the form was distorting and made clear popping noises like there was a war raging inside of her. A low growling rolled over to where I laid frozen. The smoky figure started to reach forward to my son. I threw the blankets off and rushed to the crib, gathering him up into my arms and holding him tight. As I stood next to whatever the mass was, I had no choice but to meet their gaze and look into that cold blackness. I wanted to scream. I wanted to tear my hair out and scratch out my eyes to break the connection.

Instead, the creature opened their mouth and out ripped a shriek so loud that I barely registered as a high-pitched siren. The room vibrated, and the carpet snapped into fire like it had been hit by lighting. The greedy fingers of flame caught the end of my long sleep shirt, and the back clung to my spine in cotton strips.

I turned like I was running through corn syrup and ran down the hallway. I saw a ladder hanging from the ceiling and realized it was up to the attic. I ran towards that, wanting to hide from the demon's fire and insane visions. As I struggled to climb with one arm, my son thrashed. I leaned down to comfort him.

I screamed and dropped him when I realized it wasn't my son at all, but a wooden dummy of a child. Twisted red lips were drawn on in a haphazard sweep, a thin wooden chest heaving, robotic arms and legs jerking. But the eyes were human and froze me in place, calling me towards it. Wanting me to look past the demon doll features and accept it as my own.

"I'm okay, Mommy. You saved me. You saved me," I heard coming from the dummy's mouth as if on loop.

A scream filled the room once more. Terry was shaking me awake. "Claire, stop. It's just a dream."

I woke up once again and saw that I was back in the beach house. The sheets tangled around me and the early morning sun streamed through the open window.

"Hey, it's okay," Terry said, wrapping me in her arms and settling in next to me.

"I'm sorry, I didn't mean to wake you up. I had a nightmare."

"Yeah, I caught that. It's okay."

I thought about my dream, the Terry shape standing at the foot of my child's bed. I didn't want to be afraid of my sister. My whole life she has been my comfort in a world that was confusing and huge. Or, she used to be before the accident, and these past memories overtook our life. We tiptoed around each other now, unsure of how to move on. But here, Barbara was far away. When I hugged my sister, I felt her spirit alone.

Crying quietly, I let myself melt into her breastbone, she patted my back and shushed me until I fell back asleep.

She must have been terrified like this all the time, relieved when she found that there was only one voice in her head. But she gave her comfort to me, just like she always did.

*

"Someone's going to have to cook at some point," Terry yawned.

While she stretched the blanket drifted back over to her side and Macy and I yanked it back.

We had been having a Bring it On marathon in Macy's room, where the one TV in the house was located for some reason. Macy's snacks had lasted most of the day, but if I thought about eating one more cookie, I was going to be sick. But I also had no urge whatsoever to leave the comfort of the blanket hot pocket to venture into the cold kitchen.

"I wonder if we could order pizza and have them just bring it straight to us," I said.

Macy nodded. "Yeah. I thought of that too, but I remember Terry locking the door before we went to bed."

"Damn your practicality," I said to Terry, laughing.

Terry nodded to the open window across the room. "We could write in the special requests to have them bring it to the window instead of the front door? Then we would just have to leave the bed for one-minute tops to pay him."

Macy laughed. "Do it."

While Terry ordered pizza on her phone, the baby rolled around enthusiastically. He was getting so strong that his jabs took my breath away. I focused my mental energy on calming him and hummed a little lullaby. Macy patted my belly, and Terry smiled at us. All connected that way, a jolt of warm energy rolled through me and gasped. I saw a swirling royal blue light dancing behind Macy's head. Shocks of purple were weaved through it like glitter.

"What?" she said, turning.

Her mouth dropped open, and Terry's eyes widened comically.

"What is that?" I asked, gaping at her.

"An aura!" Macy said, ecstatic to share it with us.

I had been able to project my gift throughout my whole pregnancy, but holding my sister's hand and thinking about the baby seemed to have let me project Macy's gift as well. I had imagined what auras looked like before but never could have pictured how magical they really were.

"Whose?" Terry asked.

"They are usually by the person's head. It's behind me, it must be mine. Claire, I have always wanted to see my aura. It's beautiful. And… it matches Britney's perfectly," Macy said, her voice cracking a little bit.

"Could you try to see his?" I asked.

Macy turned back to me, her face lighting up. Trusting each other to work on our gifts and share them with each other was so comforting and connected us in a way nothing else had the power to do.

We watched her cover her face with one hand and lay the other on my stomach. Little by little, wisps of gold started to twinkle around my belly. My son rolled with the color, and the gold and flecks of silver seemed to dance in response. It was the most beautiful gold I had ever seen. This was different than an ultrasound, this felt like my son communicating with me directly. I thought back to Macy telling me that my aura was green and wondered what that meant.

Macy brushed tears off her cheek. "Gold means that you are being mentored and protected beyond yourself. That you are being watched over by divine beings, angels."

I held her cheek, overcome with such a gift. Our lives might have been hectic right now, and I was scared for my child. But, my mom had our back. Whoever gave us these gifts in the first place was watching over this new beautiful life growing inside of me. We were going to be okay.

"What?" a voice at the window made me jump, and the connection was broken.

The colors disappeared from the air, but it was clear the projection had reached our very stunned pizza man. Terry hopped out of bed and gave him a twenty-dollar bill.

"Keep the change," Terry said.

She took the pizza and shut the window and blinds while we laughed on the bed.

*

Our trip had barely lasted three days, but we still found time for shopping and buying a bunch of seashell encrusted things we probably didn't need. I took out a photo frame lined with shells and glitter and put it into a paper bag for Ash.

"Anything in there for me?" I heard from behind me.

I jumped and spun to see Len stretched out on my bed. My skin crawled. I turned away from him, focusing on blocking him out. Setting up boundaries in my meditation was impossible, forcing him away wasn't going to work. But I still had to try. Every time I saw him, more memories came back.

"No. Go away, Len," I said, breathing deeply to stay calm.

Getting upset seemed to give him more power. I heard him stand and walk over to me. When he was close enough to reach out to me, I stiffened and imagined a thick wall.

He laughed. "It's pointless. We are connected. No wall will keep me away, and no boyfriend either. You belong to me, Claire."

His fingers brushed my shoulder, and I pushed him away. "That doesn't mean anything to me. I am not yours; I am my own. I am Holden's."

Len grabbed my shoulders and forced me around to look at him.

"Is that right? I can take care of that; I can take care of him. Is he planning on moving in? I like that plan the most. In that case, it's so easy to just watch and wait until you think I am gone. Until you are back to sleeping without listening to the creaks in the house. I could easily just take a pillow and put it over his head. I could make you mine again."

His palm covered my mouth, and he forced a vision into my mind. Holden struggling under Lens weight with one of my pillows pressed against his mouth and nose. His hands flailed as he fought for air.

A scream fought its way up and shrieked through his fingers. Len laughed and clamped his lips against mine, holding me in place as he kissed me despite my thrashing. His kissed forced even more disgusting visions into me, but these weren't threats. These visions were of things that I had forced myself to forget.

Len talking me into touching him, telling me that I was special and that he would love me regardless of my gift. That he would love me because of my gift. He talked me through tears and guided me when I hesitated. I saw him coaxing me out of my shirt and touching my still developing chest. Whispering promises, whispering consequences.

I concentrated all my energy into my body until it was barely contained and threw him away from me. He hit the wall and seemed to splash into mist but he was still simpering. He believed he still had so much control over me.

But I refused to be his victim. I refused to let him do this to my body while I was growing another one inside of me. This ended now because I was stronger. If Terry could find the strength to fight against an entire other life contained inside of her, I was strong enough to defeat my demons as well.

*

"What's this?" Ash asked, pulling a huge poster board from the coffee table and holding it up.

I grinned at her. "I think that our trip gave Macy the little nudge she still needed. Yesterday she stood in front of the school with that to ask Britney to Prom."

"In front of the whole school? Exactly the gesture Britney needed."

I nodded. "It worked, of course. What girl could resist that. They were over last night watching movies and being more nauseating than usual."

The projections had still been sharp, and I had been able to see the moment from Macy's perspective. When Britney saw her and realized what she was doing, how big it was, this look came over her face was hard to describe. Perfect contentment was the closest word that came to mind. She kissed my sister, and it all just clicked. They were meant to be, and Macy would always be loved.

"Good for them."

"It was nice to see her happy," I said, giving her what Missy left behind.

"Where did Missy get these?" Ash asked, holding a tube of sage and other herbs.

"I have no idea. I didn't ask. She just said they would work," I said, getting the lighter out of the kitchen drawer where Terry kept extra candles for power outages.

We had used sage on the house before, but it wasn't strong enough to keep a spirit as strong as Barbara out for long. However, this time I was using it for Len.

"Is this all we have to do? Burn this?"

"No. I need you to visualize white light filling the rooms as well. She said to let the sage relax you and allow it to fill your psyche and environment with cleaning energy."

"What will you do?" she asked, lighting the sage and doing an experimental swirl with it.

I took a letter out of my back pocket. It shook slightly in my sweaty grip.

"I have to confront Len."

She smiled at me slightly and leaned in to hug me. I inhaled deeply and took one last breath of her perfume, gaining strength from it.

"We can do this," Ash said, brandishing her smudging stick like a sword.

I nodded and opened the letter. Len didn't need to be here for this to work, but I had a feeling he would show up at some point.

"Len. I know that you think that we had some great love affair and for a long time that's what I let myself believe. I believed that you were my first love, the person I trusted with my first kiss and my secrets. You knew exactly what I needed to hear and you said it to gain my trust. When you disappeared, I was devastated. But being back and being an adult has let me see those memories in a completely new light. I can now see that maybe I made myself forget the truth of those memories because it was easier to believe that things unfolded the way they did because I loved you."

My skin prickled and I saw Len standing by the kitchen doorway. Smirking at the sage, acknowledging that this wouldn't work unless I was firm in my decision. He still thought he was able to confuse me, make me do what he wanted. But I wasn't a little girl anymore.

"But I didn't love you. I was afraid of you. And you didn't love me. You met a girl destroyed by her parent's divorce and confused about a gift she was afraid of. You took advantage of

266

that and groomed me. You gained my trust, and you exploited it. You kissed me and took me further than I ever should have gone. When you touched me, you betrayed me. When you forced me to touch you, you destroyed me. When I think of those days, locked in your embrace and unsure of why I felt ashamed, I am nauseated. You disgust me."

Lens smirk faltered. He tried to speak, but I was so focused that I was able to silence him. He would never be able to give me his excuses and his side of the story because I knew the truth.

I didn't need an apology. I needed my voice. He would never silence me again.

"You hurt me, but you will never hurt me again. You are not welcome in this home, in my memories. What happened to Rusty wasn't your fault, and for a long time, I let you use it as an excuse for what you did to me. But I have met Rusty, and he was a better person than you will ever be. You disrespected his memory in so many ways. You became someone he would have hated; you gave into the darkness. Goodbye Len. I hope you pay for what you did."

I tried stepping back and separating myself from Len and what he had done to me. He sauntered over and grabbed my arms, silently screaming into my face as he tried to hold on. But I held onto my power, to the electricity trickling through my body. I thought of those days at the lake and one by one, I forgave myself. I cried as the weight in my heart got lighter. Len was solid now. I peeled his fingers from my arm, saying goodbye. Refusing to be touched by him ever again, in my head, in my heart.

As the sage began to clear, Len seemed to evaporate with it. With my resolution and my reconciliation with these memories, he no longer had any power. He didn't have anything to hold onto anymore. I was free.

I collapsed onto the ground, the still hot end of the smudging stick burning my thigh slightly. Ash dropped to the ground in front of me, hugging me and crying with me.

"I am proud of you. You did so well," she said, rubbing my back and bringing me back.

I cried for a long time. Crying for that little girl who was so scared that she trusted a monster. Grieving for the teenager who repressed those memories to save herself. Crying from the relief of not having to carry it around with me in this new stage of my life.

Terry

Ash had been so kind about letting me stay and not making a big deal about why I wasn't at home with my sisters. But it was time to come home. We had a baby shower lunch the night before, and Ash's mom had wholly ignored the no gifts invitation and gone all out. It was going to take two trips to move back in.

I held the considerable car seat box against my hip and tried to shimmy the trunk open with my sneaker.

"Can I help?" I lowered the box to see who was standing in the yard, expecting Holden.

A lanky guy with blue eyes and shaggy black hair looked at me curiously. I saw how he appeared in front of me but was dizzy with another image superimposing itself in front of him. A brown crew cut and a jawline that looked like it was cut from steel, eyes that were somehow gray and green at the same time.

"Kerry?" I gasped, almost swooning under the weight of seeing him and the box I was holding.

He laughed a little. "Eli, actually. But yes."

Eli gently hoisted the box into his own arms. I invited him inside as if walking through a hallucination. I knew that I was staring at him and acting like a crazy person but was also completely unable to stop myself.

"Well, talking about coming here and actually being here is two different things. I feel pretty weird," he said, swaying on his feet.

I let out a breath, smiling at him. "Yeah. Me too. It's hard to describe. I couldn't stop thinking about you coming and being here for me to touch...."

Eli looked up at me, and I blushed deeply. He was beautiful, here and then. What if I didn't meet his expectations? What if this version of myself was a disappointment?

"Me too, it's all I think about," he said, timidly standing closer to me.

He was a little bit taller than me, and I had to look up to make eye contact. Through him, I knew that he saw both of us, Barbara and me. Our images blending and becoming something that he also thought was beautiful. I saw the yearning and the confusion. I saw what he had been through the last couple of months trying to explain these visions, these feelings about someone who was essentially a complete stranger. I also saw the love that was still there after all these years, the passion that had survived.

"It's crazy? Right?" I whispered.

"Not to me," Eli said, closing the space between us and kissing me.

I had dreamed of this moment for months but wasn't prepared for the implosion happening in my chest. It wasn't like just kissing one person and feeling that one sensation. It was the past memories fighting their way to the surface and melding a million yesterday kisses with the one happening now. I was making out through a kaleidoscope of dimensions and not really here at the same time.

I led him somehow to my bedroom downstairs. The fierceness of how much I wanted him threatened to rip me to pieces. I tore off my shirt, and he gently knocked me onto the bed. He vibrated with his two images, a smile and grimace fighting to take control of his features. I had to squint but was able to make out a little blood on his shirt. But before I was able to react, he was above me again. Kissing my neck and collarbone, sending me into that dizzy headspace again.

I took a deep breath to keep the room from spinning and tried to concentrate on the Eli in front of me. Feeling like I was falling through a rip in space was turning my stomach despite the intense pleasure. With my eyes closed, I was able to tap into whatever psychic energy was keeping me sane.

The rational part of my mind fought to gain control. This wasn't supposed to be happening, it went wrong once.

You killed him! Don't you remember that? He betrayed you. When you tried to hurt his pregnant wife, he turned on you. You locked yourself in their bedroom and murdered him.

I remembered that part more than I really wanted to. I had slid one of the kitchen knives into my purse when sneaking into the house. As we fought, it ended up in my hand. I had caught Kerry off guard and knocked him down, pinning him with my knees on his biceps. In a crazed frenzy, I plunged the knife into his chest over and over. I stopped when my arm became stiff with blood and tired from exertion.

But was it really crazed? Tell yourself the truth. You were aware of what was happening as soon as you stabbed him the first time. It was so clear it seemed like slow motion. His face was twisted in shock and pain. You savored it. Every single slice.

I rolled to my side, suddenly needing to vomit. Eli sat up, confused.

"What's wrong?" he asked.

I shook my head. "This whole past memory thing has been really hard on my family. My sisters don't fully understand, and we share this house. This is not how I want to introduce you to them. I need some time to explain it to them. Where are you staying?"

"The Hilton by the mall," he said, steadying his breathing and raking his fingers through his hair.

"Can I call you there later? When I have had a chance to figure this all out?" I asked, not wanting him to go but needing to be alone regardless.

He nodded, and we made our way back upstairs. Watching him drive away, I felt intense relief I didn't understand. Being two people in one body was simply too much. It was beyond human comprehension. Seeing him was forcing me to add the last puzzle piece. If Eli was here, I had to honestly confront what happened to him. I had to face what happened to me.

Barbara seemed to relish that idea and the force of the vision she landed me sent me to my knees.

I was still covered with blood when I opened the bedroom door. Rachel, already swollen with pregnancy, held a gun in my direction. When she saw Kerry laying on the ground behind me, she began screaming. I watched her with amusement. She didn't love Kerry enough to kill me.

"You're pathetic," I said, ripping the gun from her and casually leaving her in the room with the bloody mess.

I walked downstairs, toying with the gun. It was so clear now. What did I have left with Kerry gone? What was the point? I heard sirens in the distance and played with how to finish this once and for all. I slid the barrel of the gun into my mouth and shook away the traitor tears that threatened to overtake me. I would be with Kerry again. This was the only way.

I screamed, spitting out the gunpowder that seemed to fill my mouth. I was okay, I was alone. This was Barbara's plan all along, to end up with Kerry and a fresh second chance. But how powerful were those memories? Would we just repeat history? Did we really deserve another shot at this?

*

"The smudging was very successful, but you never know," Missy said.

She kissed Claire and giving her two smudging sticks to keep in our junk drawer just in case.

I felt terrible that I was so removed from her life this year that I had no idea how much she was struggling with Len. I might have been able to help. She hugged Missy then her and Ash headed out for one last prenatal yoga class before her due date.

"How are you doing being back home?" Missy asked.

She asked, but she was a much stronger empath than she let on. She already knew the answer and was worried.

"It's been a little bit of a struggle," I told her. My cell phone vibrated and I sent yet another call from Eli to my voicemail. I prayed that he wouldn't show up again until I got all of my thoughts together.

Missy nodded to my phone on the counter. "Was it worth? The stuff of dreams?"

I didn't even ask how she knew. She always did. But I did shake my head and let myself be honest with her.

"No. At first, it was so intense that I thought it was just passion. But there was a lot of other stuff mixed in. Dark stuff, the death, and leftover rage. It made me sick. It was bigger than the love that I wanted so badly to hold onto. I am afraid of what might happen if we see each other again."

She rubbed my arms, warming me up like she had the power to snuff out the darkness that had attached itself to me.

"What do you want to do? Do you still want a life with him?"

I took a deep breath, one part of me assenting furiously. Another part fighting to gain back control.

"It doesn't feel safe…"

Missy looked troubled but unsure of how much to say.

"What?"

"Okay. I might not be as gifted a medium as Claire, but I can see the spirits at war here. I can see Barbara's wanting another chance and being okay with using you in the process.

But it's not actually you that will be living that chance, if that makes any sense. But what is even clearer is that Kerry's spirit isn't a forgiving as it seems. He is angry, completely dark with it. He might not want a reconciliation more than he wants your trust."

"My trust? What does that mean?"

Missy put an arm around me and squeezed. "He wants your guard down so that he can write his own ending. You might have been expecting love, but there's an even bigger chance that you and Eli will just burn up in the wake of the fury leftover by Barbara and Kerry. He might want revenge."

My arms broke out in goosebumps that itched like hives. "What do I do?"

She shook her head. "I don't think you can change their minds. If you let yourself become vulnerable to opening yourself up to love, you are also welcoming in all of their baggage and pain. Pain that has nothing to do with you and is poisoning your life."

I started to cry a little, exhausted from all of this push and pull between decades. I didn't do anything to deserve this.

"How do I stop her?" I whispered, unsure of how close Barbara was at the moment.

Missy brightened. "That I can help with. You have to say goodbye to Eli, for good. Letting him go will infuriate Barbara but keep you from being swept up in whatever is going to happen between them. It will end bloody if it's allowed to play out. It won't be easy, and she will fight you. But I will help you. You need to say goodbye and then help us move Barbara on."

I nodded, already feeling the war inside of me attempting to rationalize Kerry's anger and still wanting him.

"Are you ready to get your life back?" Missy asked.

I nodded, Barbara clinging to me and fighting my choice to do even that. But I was finally able to breathe.

*

I was sure of myself in the daytime hours, but when I was sleeping Barbara ultimately took over. She was so close to my consciousness that it didn't even feel like a fight. It felt like slipping into another skin I fit into perfectly. She knew that I was done with this drama. At the same time, she knew that it wasn't something she was willing to let go of yet.

I found myself walking in the night, slippers on my feet and wearing nothing but the huge black T-shirt I had worn to bed. I knocked on a hotel door. Eli answered, his hair messy from sleep and his smile beautiful. I wasn't fully asleep anymore, but I also didn't feel like I had any power to make myself walk away when all that I wanted for the past eight months was right in front of me.

"I knew you would come," he told me, drawing me in.

He wasted no time wrapping me in his arms and trailing kisses across my neck and collarbone.

"I couldn't stop myself," I told him honestly.

I laid back on the bed, and he gently pulled my shirt off. He was already shirtless and slipped out of his pajama bottoms. His skin was hot against mine, and I almost wanted to pull away. Instead, I drew him to me to the point of pain. I kissed him hard and gave him all of the confusion and anxiety I had held onto the last year. He returned it, and I reached the peak of solace.

"I loved you so much," he told me, sitting up on his elbows and looking down at me.

"You felt so far away. It's like I am complete," I told him.

He caressed my collarbone and then gripped my neck tightly. I expected to feel startled but didn't. Through him, a vision filled me from Kerry's point of view.

He wasn't sure about Rachel, I was persuasive. He had fallen in love with me despite his best efforts. He had come to the realization that he had to pick, and Barbara barely won.

But when Rachel found out she was pregnant, there was a hope in that as well. A desire for something that wasn't made from being broken. Something that was perfect all on its own. Something that belonged to him and might be a way for him to redeem himself.

Then Barbara had ruined his life. She stole from him the single dream that had ever been important to him.

I came back into myself as the oxygen was stolen from my lungs. I ripped myself from the vision and clawed at Eli's back.

This wasn't Kerry, this wasn't Barbara. I was Terry and Eli was choking me to death. We were never going to have a second chance. Barbara had stolen my life from me, had taken CJ from me. I had lost my first chance before I even realized it was in front of me. This was my proof.

I held my breath and focused all my fear into one explosive blast. I wanted another shot, I wanted to be Terry. I screamed and saw the white flash of light burst from me. Eli shot across the room and hit the wall opposite the bed. He crumpled to the ground and was still. I grabbed my shirt and yanked it over my head. On my way out of the room, I looked in the mirror and saw the already blossoming bruises encircling my neck.

I had spent my whole career telling my clients that they didn't deserve this. They didn't deserve pain, they didn't deserve violence, and they didn't deserve a love that made them hate themselves.

I already knew that the best way to love another person was to love yourself. But I also realized that I needed to find my way back to myself. It was the only way I would escape this with my life.

Chapter 13

Claire

I knew that letting go of Eli would be difficult for Terry. But I never thought we would have to go to these lengths to get rid of him. Terry had called him yesterday to ask him to go back home. He ultimately refused. He told her that she was just afraid of what they meant to each other. He told her that we were getting in the way.

Eli stayed one more night and called her again this morning. She refused the call but knew that he was on his way over. Missy gave her one look and suggested that we tied her to her a chair until this whole thing was over. I was horrified, but Terry agreed. Barbara was stronger than ever.

Eli came to the door, and Holden went outside to get him to leave. I saw him through the living room window and so could Terry. Her eyes rolled into the back of her head in rhythmic circles, and she fought against the ropes that Missy had found in the garage. A guttural growl was coming out of her throat. Seeing her fighting to get him, I didn't see how she believed that whatever Barbara wanted with him was safe.

"I'm going to help Holden, Terry. I will be right back," I leaned down to kiss her cheek and Missy grabbed my arm.

I nodded and wiped the tears from my cheeks before joining Holden outside.

"I just want to hear it from her," Eli said.

"You want to hear it from who?" I asked him.

His eyebrows furrowed. "Who else?"

"I don't know. Terry or Barbara."

When I said Barbara's name, his face clouded over.

"Terry. She is who I am here for."

He glanced at me briefly before beginning to yell at Holden again. I stepped between them, silencing him. He glared at me like he wanted to shake me but pressed his lips together tightly instead.

"That's not going to work. We are Terry's family, not Barbara's. And Barbara is killing her. Right now, my sister is tied to a chair and ripping bloody gashes into her arms to get free. She doesn't belong caught up in this mess. Barbara might have loved you when you two existed together, but there's no room for it here," I told him.

I thought the idea of my sister bloodied like that would have shocked him into silence. But for one terrible moment, he looked incredibly satisfied. I shivered as he looked at us and I was able to see the superimposing souls that Terry had described. He was Eli from California, but he was also Kerry. And Kerry wanted more than blood.

"Why did you come?" Holden asked, his fists clenched at his sides.

I realized I had been projecting and he was seeing the same sick dance of souls. More than that, we were choking on the pure rage that emanated from him.

Eli shook his head. "You would never understand. I came because I love her. I always have."

"Yet, you left her back then. And, last night you left bruises on her neck. That's not love," I said, thoroughly infuriated.

I had no idea what went on at that hotel, but she came home looking like she had been hit by a car. I didn't know if she hurt him back, I just knew that my sister was in pain and he was part of the reason.

He shrugged. "But this is a second chance. Don't you see that?"

"A second chance for what?"

Eli grinned, and it was impossibly clear. He loved her, he hated her, and this was his second chance to rewrite an ending. Including not being the one to die locked in a bathroom. Suddenly his head fell back slightly, and he gasped. When he looked at us again, his eyes seemed a shade lighter, and his face was pale.

"She had bruises on her neck?" Eli asked.

Holden's mouth fell open. Whatever hold that Kerry had on Eli seemed to be as precarious at the one that Barbara had on Terry.

"Yes," I whispered.

Eli shook his head lightly. "I never wanted any of this. My life was… normal. But then she messaged me, and it was like I woke up with someone else sharing my skin. I never meant to hurt her."

Holden nodded. "Then leave. Before this gets worse."

He looked down once more before glancing up, his eyes dark and stormy again.

"Maybe I want it to get worse."

"Get the fuck out here, now. I am going to call the cops," Holden said, stepping close to him with a look I had never seen before.

Instead of seeming intimidated, Eli stepped up to him and pushed him backward.

"You are going to make me leave? What's keeping me from just going inside and getting Terry myself?" he asked.

Holden flushed, and he pulled his fist back before connecting with Eli's jaw. The darkness in Eli's eyes seemed to blacken them, and he jumped at Holden. They fell to the ground, punching and rolling. I screamed for them to stop, seeing black spots as I saw his just healed arm hit the pavement savagely. Eli rolled on top of Holden and punched him over and over.

As I screamed again, my fear seemed to project outwards and absorb a piece of the anger that surrounded Eli. I saw him punching Eli, but I was also sent visions of him choking Terry to death like vibrations. I could see her empty expression as he slid a knife beneath her rib cage. I saw how this would end, how it would always end.

Holden launched Eli off of his chest and rolled, pinning him. Just as he was about to hit him again, all the light seemed to leave Elis features. Holden's fist froze in the air as Eli looked around wildly.

"Eli?" I asked.

He locked his gaze on mine, the visions seeming to have awakened what was left of his control.

"I'll leave, but I can't guarantee he won't come back," he gasped.

Holden stood, and Eli scrambled to his feet. Eli suddenly laughed shrilly but walked back to his car. He squeezed the steering wheel, and he seemed to be arguing with himself. I hoped that whatever this supernatural bond was would disappear once we moved Barbara on. It wasn't natural, and it was ruining two innocent lives.

I went to Holden, touching the already bruised brow above his right eye. He took my fingers and kissed them.

"It's fine."

Holden stamped a kiss on my forehead and steered me back inside. Terry was slumped in the chair, breathing heavily. Missy sat in front of her, the lines of her shoulders weary and tired.

"Is she okay?" I asked, dropping to my knees to gently tip her chin up.

"Yes. Barbara is exhausted for now. As soon as she loosened her grip, I cast a protective circle over Terry. It won't hold forever, but will do for now," Missy told me.

She brushed Terry's hair back from her forehead.

I took a deep breath, holding my belly. "Okay, good. Because my water just broke."

*

I was a couple weeks early, but our little one was already strong and ready to come home. After a frantic drive to the hospital, Missy had left us to pick up Macy from a friend's house and brought her to us. I was getting ready to dress in that terrible hospital gown when Holden surprised me with a light cotton nightgown.

"My mom bought this for you. She said that it brought her so much comfort and she wanted you to have that," he said, smiling.

The nightgown was light purple with yellow daisies. I could tell she spent time picking it out and wiped my cheeks. I took it gratefully and settled into the bed. The nurses put in an IV and checked my blood pressure. I was ready for hours and hours of waiting but confronting your sister's murderous spirit boyfriend did wonders to speed things up.

My doctor was poised between my legs and told me to get through this last contraction, then I would start to push. I was excited and terrified. Holden held one of my legs, and my sisters were clenching the bed railing on either side of me. Their faces were shiny with expectation and pure joy. As they all touched me and concentrated on the future with me, I was able to look into each one of them. The pain coursing through my body seemed to lay me open, and I was able to receive it all.

The nervousness and giddiness from Macy. How me and Holden made her believe in a love that was able to overcome any obstacle. The pride and slight envy from Terry. How much she wanted to start a family and give me the gift of nieces and nephews. The protectiveness and how hard it was for her to see me writhing in agony. And Holden, I saw this moment through him.

When I began pushing, and our son started to make his gory and fantastic debut into the world, I saw how his world seemed to freeze for a second. He fell in love on the spot. I saw all his dreams of the future. He took one moment to look up at me, and I felt his devotion and how it deepened when confronted with the life that we had created together. Being the mother of his child was the biggest honor. I wanted it all.

My doctor stepped back a little, and our little boy slid into Holden's arms. He let Terry cut the cord and then carried him over to gently lay him on my chest. His eyes were golden brown, and he already had a messy mop of soft brown hair. He was crying lightly until his skin settled against mine. He blinked up at me.

"Hi, little one," I whispered, rubbing his back and crying quietly.

"Noah," Holden whispered.

I looked up at him in wonder. "Noah?"

"It's what I have been calling him for months. I stayed over in January, and I seemed to wake up with it like he told it to me. It sounded right."

I nodded and put my lips to his cheek, telling him his name. "Noah Holden."

My sisters kissed Noah and took a million photos before the nurse notified us that Holden's parents had arrived. Terry and Macy kissed us one last time before making room for the new grandparents.

"Holl, before they get here, I wanted to ask you something," I said, sitting up and cradling Noah between us.

"Do you need something? Are you thirsty?"

"No," I laughed.

"Just listen."

Holden grinned and sat next to me on the bed.

I wore a sapphire class ring on my thumb. My mom had accidentally ordered it too big, but I loved it too much to send it back. Holden used to tease me about wearing it on my thumb like Criss Angel, but now the size seemed predestined. I slid it off my thumb and gently slipped it onto Holden's ring finger, threading our fingers.

"You don't have to keep that. You can pick out your own manly ring if you want to. But you do have to marry me," I told him, kissing him on the cheek with Noah snoozing on my chest and Holden's fingers clasped around his impossibly small foot.

Holden rolled his eyes and laughed a little. "Pots and rings meant for women. When are you going to get this present thing figured out?"

I laughed and smacked him away. He caught my hand and kissed it before pulling me closer and kissing me on the lips. Holden rested his forehead against mine, and I felt him again, coursing through me with love that was too big to contain in my body. Love tangled together with the love he had for our son and the family we became together.

"It's always been yes, Claire. It's always been you."

*

Missy had cast the most powerful circle of protection I had ever seen, it still glowed with promise. But I was still nervous leaving Holden and Noah here. Holden's parents' house was perfect and miles away from my home, but it was still terrifying leaving my child even for just a couple hours.

"Are you sure it will work? Nothing will be able to get in?" I asked her.

She nodded for the millionth time. Holden laughed quietly to avoid waking our son, who was sleeping in his crib.

"It will be fine. Noah's going to have a nap. I am going to finish this book. You will be back in an hour," he said, kissing me on the forehead.

"Are you sure?" I asked him, searching his expression for fear.

There was none. He trusted Missy, he trusted me.

Holden nodded firmly and pushed me towards the door. "Go clean house."

The drive back to my house was tense. Missy ran through her list of things to do once more and warned me of all the things that might go wrong. She tried to warn me that Terry might not have the strength to reclaim her body. That she might become lost in the middle ground that she resided in while in her coma. But what was the alternative? She was losing her mind already. Barbara was intent on destroying anything that was organically Terry. I owed this to her, regardless of the risks.

I closed the front door tightly and followed Missy downstairs where Macy and Terry were waiting. We set up the den with white candlelight for protection and Missy cast another circle around us so that nothing could leave this room. Seeing Mac through the candle smoke reminded me of that night at the lake when we moved Caroline on. I still had nightmares of that night. Just thinking of Caroline becoming engulfed in flames made me shiver. Macy seemed to be thinking of the same thing and gave me a quick hug before sitting next to Terry.

"I don't think this is going to look pretty. You have to promise to keep going no matter what I say," Terry said, her face ashen with fear.

I nodded but was already crying.

"Tell them the idea you had," Missy said, sitting outside the circle to keep an eye on her protection casting.

"I know this is going to sound crazy, but I think this our best chance to really clean all the bad energy out once and for all. Throughout my pregnancy, I have been able to project and kind of absorbed your gifs at one point or another. I think that's the key. Your gifts don't have any power over Barbara or the shadow figures here, but there's a chance they will give mine more power," I said, nervously.

Terry, despite her best intentions, looked at me suspiciously.

"You want us to will our powers to you?" Macy asked, confused.

"Not forever. I want to borrow them to cast Barbara away. I don't know if I can do it on my own."

"Will we get them back?" Terry asked.

I blushed; it was asking too much. But we didn't really have another choice.

290

"I don't know."

They thought quietly for a moment before Macy nodded.

"It's to keep us safe. If we are meant to keep them, we will. If not, then I guess we aren't meant to keep them," she said, looking a little tearful.

These were also a connection to Mom and what her memory truly meant to us.

Terry was fully crying but nodded. "I trust you."

We held hands and as we formed a circle of power. Barbara quickly emerged from within Terry, where I figured she had truly lived for months now. Terry dug her nails into me and looked at me with pure hate, Barbara rolling her eyes back again.

Macy gasped, and her power burned through my arm, melding with my own and creating a colorful hurricane. Missy walked around the circle. She laid down agate and emerald stones, praying under her breath. She might have been psychic and be able to call upon the strength of sage and crystals, but she believed wholeheartedly in a divine spirit. Seeing all she had done for this; I was beginning to believe in some kind of divine intervention myself. A white bubble seemed to encase us.

"I surround us with a shield of protection. We are safe within this space," I said, firmly.

Barbara laughed through Terry and Macy's skin broke out in goosebumps.

"Any unwanted spirits and entities leave now. Leave this space. You don't belong here. I am sending you home. Go back whence you came. Leave now. Only light and healing energy are allowed in this room," I said, encouraging Macy to talk along with me.

Terry started to writhe, and her limbs twitched with panic. Macy's spirit and power coursed through me and searched for Terry. She was either holding back, or Barbara was refusing to let her help us.

"Terry, please. For me, please help me. Let me set you free," I whispered to her.

She shook her head violently, and I was afraid Barbara would break her neck before letting her go. A laugh rocked through her chest, and she was sweating heavily. Instead of scaring me, I was beyond angry. We had been through so much. Terry had been through so much. She didn't deserve this. I promised I would save her; it was my turn to protect her.

I gripped Macy's hand tighter and asked her to keep repeating the protection incantation. Then I looked into myself and sought out Barbara. She was in the shadowland, half reaching into my sister as if it was as easy as playing a game. The shadow figures crawled towards me, but I was still encased in light. As I got close to Barbara, walking became harder and harder. Finally, I reached her and used all of my strength to rip her from my sister, screaming with the effort.

Terry slumped, the movement forcing my eyes open. A gasp ripped from my chest as I realized that Terry wasn't alone anymore. Our mom stood behind her with another woman with light auburn hair. Her features were gently lined, and she peered down at us with such love.

"Grandma?" I whispered.

Terry looked over her shoulder, and Mom nodded to her. Macy's mouth dropped open, and she reached out to our family, her eyes locked on our grandma.

"You have to fight, baby. This won't work unless you love yourself enough to hold on. Barbara doesn't deserve a second chance, but you do. You are worth it, you are beautiful, and you are powerful. Let Claire help you, my love," my mom told her, vibrating with gold waves.

The waves were the exact same shade of Noah's aura. She was the one who had been protecting him, storing up her power until we needed her.

Terry was crying but seemed to get ahold of herself for the first time in months. She slowly stood up and looked at me, inexplicably tired but finally filled with complete trust for the first time. I called out as her vast power jolted through me, almost overtaking my own. It built inside of me as Terry dropped my hand and got on her knees. She was in control now and started to heave, blood coming out her mouth in spurts. I was shocked but not surprised that Barbara would have this kind of physical form, poisoning my sister like cancer.

When she was finally finished, we reestablished our circle, this time joined by my mom and grandma Carla. I concentrated on the blood and closed my eyes. In the shadowland, Barbara had taken on her death state. She was close to losing control completely. She screamed and fought to overtake Terry again. She had waited so long, she wasn't finished.

I filled the shadowland up with light so complete that the single dark place left was inside of Barbara. The shadow figures were confused but still hungry. They followed the blackness into Barbara, tearing her apart as they sought out their dark meal. I opened my eyes and saw the blood slowly turning to ash, twisting itself and beginning to pulse with the pain and anger contained within it.

"Get out of the circle," I whispered to my sisters.

They crawled out, exhausted. Missy tossed me a small vial of holy water. I sprinkled it over the ash, flinching at the noises emanating from it. Last, she passed me a lighter, and I set the whole mess aflame.

The bubble of protection held it as I crawled out. We watched the ash fight against the holy fire until it just seemed to implode on itself. A huge scream, intertwined with Barbara and the thousands of shadow figures she had brought her, rocked the room. And then it was gone. They were all gone.

"Look who it is," Holden said.

He pointed over the gate, where my dad was standing with a gift bag.

It was finally beautiful enough outside to grill, which was perfect for celebrating Macy's graduation from high school. She and Britney had been playing in the clubhouse all afternoon, and Holden grilled. It felt just like that first Fourth of July we had together, except now we had Terry back.

Terry glanced at me, and I followed her over to the gate.

"Hi, Dad," Terry said wearily.

The last time we talked, we had been trying to get him on board to help Macy press charges, and we got into another huge fight. For the first time, I saw things from his point of view in the form of a vision. He was terrified of losing us just like he lost our mom, but he blamed the visions. We couldn't change who we were, and it was time he accepted that.

"Hi, I brought a gift," he said, raising the gift bag up.

"I think that will be okay. But Macy's girlfriend is here. I want to make sure you aren't here to ruin her graduation party."

My dad looked ashamed of himself and a little angry, but he was finally seeing that this was the only way we were going to have a future together.

"I think it's time we met," he said finally.

Terry opened the gate and ushered him into the yard. Macy saw us coming over and wrapped an arm around Britney's waist. I knew a part of her wanted to rub this in our dad's face and an even more significant part of her wanted this to the moment she always dreamed of.

"Hey Mac, happy graduation."

She looked at us, unsure of whether or not to be happy or upset.

"Thank you. This is my girlfriend, Britney."

Britney grinned and stuck out her hand. "Nice to meet you, sir."

I turned slightly to hide my smile. He looked shocked for a moment, either at how happy Macy was when with Britney or by how normal this all could be if he let his guard down.

"It's a pleasure to meet you," he said, shaking her hand.

Macy's bottom lip trembled, and she stepped forward to hug him. I saw my dad wipe his cheeks discreetly before he straightened and turned to me.

"I think there's someone else I have yet to meet."

And life was perfect because this was the dad I had grown up with. The dad who helped me with my homework and read the very first stories that I wrote. I wished more than anything he could be this person for Macy and Terry. Maybe this really was a second chance, for all of us.

"Of course, Dad. Come meet your grandson, Noah."

Terry

May 2016

Claire had told me that CJ came to visit her while I was setting back up at work, which hurt more than I wanted to admit. If he was visiting while I was gone on purpose, things really had become more broken than I had allowed myself to believe. When I thought about the last year and the limbo that CJ has been hanging in, I was ashamed of myself.

I let myself get so lost. I hoped it wasn't too late. I felt like I needed to send out the best vibes to the universe because I needed it sorely. I sent him a text message to meet me at Sally's at 10 pm that night. It was already 10:15 and our fries were getting floppy, but I would sit here all night if it came to it.

"I hope you bought two of those. Last time I barely got two sips," CJ said, sitting down beside me and gesturing to the fudge milkshake in the center of the table.

"You can have it all," I said, gratefully pushing it towards him.

He smiled cautiously and held it but didn't take a drink.

"CJ..." I started, but he shook his head.

"If this is you telling me that he came to see you and that you are following him to California, please just don't. I can't hear it," he said, his voice breaking.

My mouth dropped open. Is that what he thought of me? That I would bring him to our special place to break that kind of news to him? That this is where I would leave him forever? How cruel did he think I was?

"I sent him away. I don't even know if Barbara really was my past life or if she just was able to make me believe she was because I was weak after waking up. With my mom gone, I felt like a failure and didn't know how to start over. I let myself get so lost."

CJ looked up, not wanting to be hopeful.

"I know."

"I thought it would be easier, but it was the worst thing I have ever done. A life without you isn't a life I want to be part of."

He fiddled with the straw of his drink. "As a friend?"

I laughed and laced my fingers behind his neck gently. When he looked up, I knew that all of the broken pieces of my heart weren't beyond repair. When I looked at him, reincarnation finally made sense, because one forever wasn't enough.

"Hell no."

If you enjoyed meeting the Shaw Sisters in Strangers in the Shadows…You won't want to miss the next chapter of their lives in the last installment of the Shaw Sisters Trilogy

Screams in the Forest

Coming to paperback and e-book the fall of 2019.

Read on for a sneak peek!

About the Author

Nita Farris is a freelance writer and author of SNEAKERS IN THE WATER and STRANGERS IN THE SHADOWS. She lives in Washington with her husband and two children. Keep an eye out for the last installment of the Shaw Sister Trilogy, SCREAMS IN THE FOREST, coming out the fall of 2019.

Twitter: @farrisjuanita

Instagram: @nitafarrisauthor

www.ingramcontent.com/pod-product-compliance
Lightning Source LLC
Chambersburg PA
CBHW020339180626
46812CB00001B/260